Scotti   The Bay of Na _ 19 (

THE BAY OF NAPLES

Alan Clews

Polygon

1752733 ᆨ

First published in 2009 by Polygon,
an imprint of Birlinn Ltd

West Newington House
10 Newington Road
Edinburgh
EH9 1QS

www.birlinn.co.uk

9 8 7 6 5 4 3 2 1

ISBN 978 1 84697 110 5

British Library Cataloguing-in-Publication Data
A catalogue record for this book is available on request from the
British Library.

Typeset by SJC
Printed and bound by Athenaeum Press Ltd., Gateshead, Tyne & Wear

For Sam

The man was seated at one of the small tables against the far wall of the café.

He had unscrewed the top of a grey army-surplus petrol can and was pouring petrol from it, with great care and deliberation, over himself. Crossland, who owned the café, stood motionless in front of him, trying to take in what he was seeing.

The man raised the can and let the liquid splash gently over his head. He was utterly absorbed in what he was doing, like a priest performing some obscure, complicated ritual. The petrol gleamed in his hair and ran in spiky, purposeful trickles down his face and neck, darkening his shirt collar. He kept his face tilted slightly upwards so that the liquid stayed out of his eyes. The petrol was soaking greedily into the heavy blue cloth of his overcoat.

1

Like many other Italians, Franco Giaconelli came to Scotland in the early 1930s. Franco had been born and had grown up in Pozzuoli, which lies on the northern edge of the Bay of Naples. Pozzuoli is a quiet, neglected little town. A series of sun-bleached placards, which stand at intervals along the beach, provide exact figures to the third decimal place for the amount by which the level of the land has slipped into the sea for each year since 1951. The last date given is now some years ago and no one has bothered to change the figures, or the placards, since.

In the 1930s, two things were likely to strike the visitor to Pozzuoli: the sense of poverty and the dust. The dust was a fine shroud on the cars, on the road, on the buildings, on the leaves of the trees. The sense of poverty was equally pervasive and equally inescapable. So it's not difficult to understand why Franco, in his late teens, with his mother recently dead of TB and his father long gone to the factories in the north, was keen to leave and find a better life somewhere else. Almost anywhere else.

When Franco first came to Britain, he hopped around – in his own words – like a flea. At various times, and usually only for a few weeks or months, he lived and worked in London,

Walsall, Leeds, Harrogate, Lytham St Annes and Edinburgh. No one, Franco included, was very clear on how he ended up in Paisley. But on that first close and humid evening, when he stepped out of the station onto the still-wet cobbles of County Square, he somehow felt that he could make a life for himself here. He quickly found a job in an Italian café on the Glasgow Road. He worked hard and kept his eyes open, learning how the business operated. After a year or so, he found a building in Albert Street that was up for sale and made an offer.

The building had been a carpet and linoleum shop that had gone bankrupt a year or two before. It had lain empty ever since. The first and second floors were living accommodation, accessed from stairs in the back shop. Over the years, the ground floor had served as a tearoom, a wine shop, a working man's restaurant, a café and much more. It never remained any of these things for very long. People would buy the building or take a lease on it, changing it to suit their own purposes each time. Then they would move on and someone else would come along, transforming it yet again. Sometimes, the owner or leaseholder would live upstairs; other times, those rooms were rented out or simply locked up and left empty. The shops nearby had also changed regularly over the years, having variously been sweetshops, bookshops, betting shops, second-hand clothes shops and so forth. Across the road there were warehouses and offices and, on the corner, a pub. On the whole, that part of Albert Street was something of a backwater but it wasn't a bad place for a café; close to the main road though not actually on it. You might not have the passing trade, but people weren't far away either and you could draw them in easy enough, if you knew how.

To buy the building, Franco borrowed money from Paulo Castelli who owned a café in Glasgow and also came from

Pozzuoli. There was nothing sentimental or fraternal in their arrangement. It was business, pure, simple and brutal. Franco couldn't borrow the money from a bank, having no security to offer, as Castelli well knew. The interest rate was a punishing thirty percent. When Franco hesitated, Castelli shrugged, 'Take it or leave it.'

Franco paid off the loan, pound by painful pound, in three years. People were surprised that he managed it so quickly, especially while he was still getting the business started. But Franco loathed owing money; as he saw it, the whole business of borrowing and lending was tainted, and dirtied the hands of both parties. There was, too, something distasteful in dealing with a leech like Castelli, Italian or not. When Franco finally handed over the last payment, he swore he'd never take another loan in his life. And he never did.

Franco was twenty-four when he took on the café; a good-looking, well set-up young man who was physically strong and had no fear of hard work. Back in Pozzuoli, Franco had played football and taken great pride in his swimming.

'Well, there was a-nothing else tae dae,' he used to say, the rhythms of his native Italian fitting inside those of his newly acquired Scottish accent like a hand in a glove.

'Nor a-nae work tae keep a boy occupied.'

When he was sixteen, he had won a famous (according to Franco) race across the Bay of Naples. There was a framed newspaper item about this race, with a photograph, which he kept on the wall in the café. The photograph showed the young Franco in his swimming costume – striped vest and droopy shorts – accepting a cup from a man with a walrus moustache and a vast contented stomach.

For the first year or so, Franco was pretty much on his own. He would hire in help when he needed it; local women to serve at the tables and wash the dishes. Otherwise, he did virtually everything himself. He made the ice cream and he served it, carving out generous creamy scoops from the big metal tubs. He made the coffee and the tea and the sandwiches. And he laid out the three-tiered cake stands that were placed on every table. These cake stands – with their pineapple fancies and strawberry tarts and empire biscuits and coconut pyramids and frangipanes and cream-filled éclairs and Savoy fingers and treacle scones and plain scones and Scotch pancakes – were quite possibly the real reason for the café's success. A few of the older people in the town still remember them with something approaching a sense of wonder, even reverence. The memory of those stands, with the fine china plates cradled in their polished silver frames and each plate laden with delights, seems to represent everything that was magical in the world of their childhood, a world that has somehow, to their great regret, long since slipped away.

At night, when the café was closed, Franco was still hard at work; cleaning the floor, polishing the tables, taking apart and washing out the big mixer he used for making the ice cream. Early in the morning, Franco was also there to take in the deliveries and get things ready for the day. He was in the café so much that people wondered if he'd ever been up to the flat or if he even knew it was there.

In the first couple of years, Franco transformed the place. He painted it, inside and out, and floored it with black and white tiles. He had the walls oak-panelled. And he put in a gleaming curved counter of oak and glass. He bought new tables and chairs and mounted a long mirror on the wall behind the counter. This mirror drew light into the café and made it seem twice as big. He fitted electric wall lights shipped over specially from Italy. These had filaments that flickered and danced like a gas flame. People loved these lights, never having seen anything quite like them before. The walls were crowded with paintings and photographs and etchings of the Bay of Naples. There were views of the bay with Vesuvius, from Vesuvius, from the south and the north; views from the sea, views of the islands, views from the islands back towards the mainland. Unsurprisingly, Franco called his café The Bay of Naples though naturally people soon shortened this to The Bay. That was its name, The Bay. And no one in the town would have been in any doubt what The Bay was or where to find it. Within a few short years, it had become part of the geography of the town, as fixed and immutable a reference point as the station or the library or the mill.

It was during those first couple of years that 'Franco' somehow but decisively became 'Frank' and 'Giaconelli' mutated into 'Jaconelli'. The new name was fine by him. It was a sign of acceptance, he said, an indication that he truly *belonged* here, that people had taken him into their hearts.

★

Early in 1937, Frank started seeing the daughter of an Italian family who owned a café on the south side of Glasgow. 'Seeing her' meant going to the family house for heavily chaperoned visits every Sunday afternoon when both cafés were closed. Frank and the girl, Antonia Rossi, were allowed roughly five minutes alone together each Sunday. When the five minutes was up, there would be a knock on the door or a cough outside and the whole family, with assorted grandparents and other interested parties, swept back into the room, eyes everywhere. Frank was fond of the Rossi girl. But he wasn't sure it was anything more than fondness. Fortunately for Frank, Antonia Rossi had some very definite ideas about her future that pretty much stopped things in their tracks before they had gone too far.

One Sunday afternoon, when the rest of the family had left them alone as usual, Antonia held Frank off with a firm hand.

'It's high time we got a couple of things straight,' she said, drawing deeply on her cigarette.

'Like-a what?' said Frank.

'Like the fact that if we dae come to an arrangement . . .'

'An arrangement?' said Frank, who was all too aware of the seconds ticking by.

'Stop that!' She clamped her hand round his wrist just as his fingers had moved onto the bare skin above her stocking. 'You know fine what I'm sayin'.'

'Can we no'-a talk once they come back?'

'Only if you want an audience of thousands.'

'Okay, okay. But let's-a be quick about it.'

'The thing is – if we come to an arrangement . . .'

'Aye,' said Frank, gazing at the clock and hoping she would get to the point quickly. Which, in all fairness to her, she did.

'I wouldn't work in the café.'

'What?' said Frank, finally turning away from the clock and relaxing his grasp on her thigh.

'I've worked plenty hard for the last God-knows-how-many years in their place,' she said, by which she meant the café owned by her parents. 'I'm no' getting married to do the same somewhere else.'

Frank looked at her.

'But it would-a be our ain place.'

She took the red-stained cigarette from her lips, exhaled the smoke in her lungs and shook her head.

'Aye, sure it would. But I'd no' be workin' in it.'

'Ours,' said Frank, thinking she might not have heard him the first time and believing absolutely that one tiny word would make all the difference to her, as it did to him.

'I'm no' jumping out of the frying pan into the fire for any man. Sorry.' But of course she didn't sound sorry.

Frank knew it was over there and then. On the whole, he felt more relieved than anything else. His only regret, he said afterwards, was that he'd wasted his last five minutes talking.

✶

Soon after Antonia Rossi exited stage left in a puff of cigarette smoke, Frank wrote to his priest in Pozzuoli. He told him, in so many words, that he was looking for a wife.

The priest knew that Frank had done well for himself. News and gossip passed from Scotland to Italy, and vice versa, with an ease and speed that sometimes beggared belief. Very little of any significance happened in the one place that wasn't known in the other soon after. The fact of Frank's success was common currency in and around Pozzuoli and had been for some time now. But, of course, that wasn't in itself enough.

Discreet enquiries were soon being made in the town about Frank's business, any debts he might have and his general prospects for the future. He was graced with visits from local priests, who would talk at length about nothing very much in particular. He was invited to tea with some of the Italian families in the town. When he went along, he was sized up like a box of tomatoes or a sack of onions by the wives, mothers and daughters while the men looked on with a mixture of unease and sympathy.

In October 1937, Frank received a letter from the priest in Pozzuoli. It was written in his customary black ink and it contained the usual terse injunctions to attend church regularly and never miss confession. Which of course Frank always meant to obey but rarely did. In this letter, the priest also mentioned a girl to whom Frank might like to write. Her name was Gina Moravia. She was twenty years old; her parents were dead and she and her sister worked at the local church school, teaching the younger children. The priest enclosed a tiny photograph of Gina, barely an inch square. It showed a serious young woman who looked more like sixteen than twenty. She had black hair and dark eyes and was wearing a cross on a simple chain round her neck. She seemed fragile, hesitant, unsure of herself. But there was no doubt that she was a very beautiful young woman. This photograph was the first sight Frank had of Gina and he carried it with him, in his wallet, cracked and creased so that you could barely make out the face any more, until the day he died.

Frank and Gina wrote to each other regularly over that winter. In March of 1938, Gina stopped writing. The priest told Frank that she had changed her mind. Frank continued to send her letters every week. But she didn't reply to any of these.

✲

One night near Easter in 1938, when the business with Gina seemed at its most hopeless, Frank was working late. The chairs were up on the tables. The floor, which he had just mopped, was still wet. Most of the lights were off.

Frank was listening to the radio that he kept in the back shop. It was tuned to a French station that was playing some relentlessly exuberant accordion music. A year or so ago, when he first started to make money from the business, he had treated himself to a second-hand Hohner. But it had hardly been out of its case since he bought it. That was one of the things he would do when he was more settled: take some lessons, learn to play it properly.

When he heard the front door open, he was on his hands and knees, humming quietly along with the music and cleaning out the refrigeration unit in the main counter. He was reaching right into the unit, wiping the condensation from the copper pipes that ran under the metal tub of ice cream. He expected any moment to hear someone call his name. Whoever it was wouldn't be able to see him from where they were standing. But no one did call out. As the silence went on, Frank thought he'd better have a look, even though the last and most-difficult-to-reach stretch of pipe wasn't yet shining like the others.

He was extracting his arm from the cabinet when a fist crashed down on the till above him. The bell rang out and the cash drawer shot open. He saw the hand grasp some of the notes as he was rising. He expected the hand to come back for more but it didn't. And when he stood up, he saw that the thief was already at the door, moving in a slightly awkward way but not running.

'Hey! What-a ye doin'?'

The thief was clearly shocked to discover that Frank had been there all the time. He started running but Frank caught him before he reached the main road. He clattered the thief against the metal grill over the newsagent's window. People from the grocery shop and the pub hurried over to help. The man neither struggled nor resisted. He was pressing the money on Frank, pleading with him to take it.

'There ye are. It's a' there. I'm sorry, Mister. I never saw you or else I'd never have tried it. Honest, I'm sorry.'

Frank ripped the money out of his hand.

'That's it. That's it a'. Honest it is,' the man was saying.

'Go on, hit him Frank. Gie him one,' someone was saying. The thief, who was about the same age as Frank, was frightened. But Frank had no intention of hitting him.

'He deserves it, Frank. Lousy bloody thief. Land one on him.'

'Scum.'

'Let's gie the bastard a doin'.'

Frank took a step backwards and slowly lifted his arm away from the man's throat.

'Let him be,' Frank said. 'I've-a got my money.'

'You want us tae phone the polis, Frank?'

'Aye,' Frank said. 'Get them round here.'

The man waited quietly, resigned and ready to take his punishment. One or two of the people round Frank poked or kicked at him. Frank held up his hand,

'I said – let him be.'

The crowd moved back.

'Keep your eye on him, Frank. Make sure he doesnae make a run for it.'

'He's no'-a goin' anywhere. Don't you worry,' said Frank. 'We're just goin' to wait here until the polis come.'

Some of the crowd drifted away then, back to the pub or the shops, sensing that the excitement was over. For the first time, Frank had a good look at the man. He was about the same height as himself, five ten or so, but thinner, less heavily built. He had a narrow, drawn face. He was unshaven and dirty. His hair was brown and his skin pale. His clothes were torn and looked as if they hadn't been changed in weeks. His left leg was shorter than his right and his left foot canted in, at an angle, towards the instep of his right foot. Which explained why Frank had been able to catch him so easily. He was strangely passive and made no attempt to escape. Nor did he try to explain himself or plead for clemency. He was simply waiting. The whole thing was out of his hands. He was powerless to affect what would happen to him here. It was as if his life was someone else's concern now.

The police van arrived fairly quickly. The sergeant, Robert Glen, knew Frank well. He was one of the people who would often call into the café after hours for a blether. Robert noted down Frank's statement while a younger policeman put the thief into the van. Frank saw the young policeman cuff the man across the head as he did so. But Frank didn't say anything. Robert told Frank the man would be in court in the morning but they wouldn't need Frank to be there. He could forget about this.

✳

Next morning, Frank was up at five thirty as usual. Everyone had heard about the robbery – the milkman, the man who delivered the bread and rolls, the woman who came with the fruit and vegetables. They all said Frank was lucky that he'd caught him and they hoped the thief would get his just desserts. Frank nodded, agreeing with them. But he'd been thinking about the man since last night – how frightened he looked, how easily he'd been caught and how resigned he'd been as he waited for the police. Frank remembered, too, how he hadn't complained when the young policeman hit him. The man had barely looked round, as if he'd expected this or at least wasn't surprised by it.

Around ten o'clock, Frank phoned the court and asked if the case had been dealt with yet. No, he was told, the man – whose name was Ian Miller – wouldn't be seen for another hour or so. The café was usually quiet at that time in the morning and Frank had a woman in to help. So he decided, after a few moments, that he would take a walk round to the court. He wasn't entirely sure why he did this. Even long afterwards, when he turned this moment over and over in his mind, he could never settle on any particular reason. He certainly wasn't motivated by revenge. That much he knew.

The court building was near the station, barely ten minutes' walk from the café. As usual, whenever Frank went anywhere in the town, he met people he knew. And the people he met all wanted to chat. But Frank didn't linger that morning, merely exchanged a few words and moved on.

Frank had never been in the court building before so it took him a while to find the right corridor. Robert Glen was outside the courtroom, waiting to be called. He was surprised to see Frank.

'What you doin' here, Frank? No need, ye know.'

'I just-a wondered what would happen.'

A man in a dark suit with a thin moustache and nicotine-stained teeth opened the double doors and nodded to Robert.

'Well, come and see. That's him up.'

Frank followed Robert into the court and took a seat beside him, near the front. There was a slight delay before Miller appeared in the dock. During this, there was some shuffling round as the solicitor and clerks dealing with the last case moved back to let those acting for Miller take their place. There was a lot of good-natured, easy banter between them. And some quiet laughter over a remark that Frank missed. When he asked Robert what he knew about Miller, Robert said that he didn't have a police record. He was from Bute but had been living on the mainland for four or five years. He'd worked in the office of a small engineering company in Greenock until recently but had lost his job when the company went bankrupt. He hadn't managed to find another job and had been living rough for the last couple of weeks.

Miller edged into the court, accompanied by a policeman, from a door at the back of the dock. His eyes rested, for a moment, on Frank. The judge said a few words to a clerk and handed him some papers. The talk in the courtroom thinned to a silence. The prosecutor gave a brisk account of the robbery. The lawyer defending Miller was a young man in a badly-fitting suit who fiddled nervously with a pencil. He didn't deny that Miller had taken the money but he made as much as he could of Miller's previous good character and recent desperate circumstances. Miller remained silent and impassive throughout this, his eyes fixed on the floor.

Robert Glen was called to the stand. Once or twice he consulted his notebook, but both questions and answers were peremptory. Nobody was in any doubt about Miller's identity or guilt.

'What'll-a happen to him, Robert?' Frank asked as the judge made some notes.

'He'll go away. Maybe six months. Probably longer with this judge.'

After a moment, Frank said,

'He never got a penny. I got it a' back. Besides, I left the door open and the place looked like it was empty.'

'Jesus, Frank. He's a thief. He deserves whatever's comin' tae him.'

'He's just-a someone down on his luck.'

'He might just never a been caught afore.'

'I know. But even so.'

Robert took a deep breath and shook his head.

'What d'you want me to do?'

'Whatever you can.'

Robert looked at Frank and saw that he was serious.

'It might no' make any difference wi' this judge.'

'Try.'

Robert went over to the prosecutor and whispered quietly to him. The prosecutor looked at Frank and waved for the lawyer for the defence to join them. The judge noticed this huddle and said, 'This had better be relevant to the case in hand. I'll no' have idle gossip in my court.'

The prosecutor rose and said it was, indeed, relevant to the case. He pointed out Frank and quickly recapped what Robert had said: no money had been lost as a result of the robbery, Frank as the café owner had been less careful than he might have been and Frank would prefer the defendant not to be harshly treated. While the lawyer for the defence added his piece, the judge stared at Frank for several seconds. He had bushy grey eyebrows and a thin beaked nose. If his expression suggested anything, it was the merest hint of irritation or possibly even of contempt. Frank wondered if maybe he should have kept quiet, after all; thought maybe he was interfering in things that were none of his concern. But it was done now.

'The man's a thief. But it's a first offence. Twenty-one days.'

He nodded, indicating that the matter was now closed. Miller looked over at Frank as he was led away. He seemed surprised but there was no indication or gesture that suggested gratitude.

'Happy, Frank?' said Robert.

'Aye, I suppose so,' said Frank. 'Thanks.'

'Don't mention it,' Robert said. Frank knew that Robert was annoyed but he didn't have time to worry about that now. It was twenty five past eleven and he was already well behind for the rush that always came just after twelve.

★

It was soon after this that Gina started replying to Frank's letters again.

Her letters came more frequently now and were less guarded. She asked about the café and the town. She wanted to know about the details of Frank's life in a way that she hadn't done before. She also started telling him more about herself and her sister and their work at the school.

At the end of September, the priest wrote to Frank and said that Gina would like to visit Scotland. She would stay with another Italian family who lived in Gourock, which the priest, having studied the map, judged to be 'far enough away, though not too far'. God's will would, he wrote, prevail. This might seem to us a strange way to arrange a marriage. But it was common enough at the time. And who's to say that marriages arranged in this way are any better or worse than those that people make for themselves? Frank certainly had no doubts about this way of managing things, then or later – though, of course, he could not have known how it would work out in the end.

★

When Gina arrived at Central Station in December 1938, Frank and the Italians from Gourock, the Ravezzis, were there to meet her. The Ravezzis were in their early sixties; their children had taken over their café near the station in Gourock and they had pretty well retired. Frank had met the old man, Joe, several times and liked him. When Gina stepped off the London train, half-carrying and half-dragging a large blue suitcase, eyes wide at the noise and commotion of people around her, Frank was the first one up the platform to meet her. He had recognised her instantly and he was beside her long before the Ravezzis joined them. He grabbed her case before they'd said a word. Then they stared at each other shyly for a moment, remembering the circumstances. Frank smiled and spoke to her quietly in Italian,

'Are you all right? Are you tired?'

'Yes,' she said, a slight flicker of panic in her eyes. She told Frank later that she thought the Ravezzis hadn't turned up, maybe didn't even exist. Frank was the only person she knew in the whole of Scotland but she didn't see how she could go home with him. What would the priest say?

'I feel like I've hardly slept since I left Pozzuoli,' she said.

'Don't worry,' Frank said. 'You'll get a good sleep tonight. Just go straight to bed when you get back.'

The talk of sleep and bed alarmed and embarrassed her. But somehow, underneath it all, she already felt safe with Frank. There was something about him she trusted: a steadiness, his smile, the decisive way he'd taken the case or perhaps some other, less easily definable quality. And now the Ravezzis reached them, Joe out of breath with the rush. Frank started to introduce them but Joe made it clear he was in charge here. Frank was happy to step back and let Joe take the lead while

Mrs Ravezzi fussed over Gina. Apart from anything, this gave him an opportunity to look at her properly for the first time. He was surprised by how small and slight she was; barely five feet, he thought, and hardly anything of her. Her skin was a smooth, light olive. Her eyes were wide, almond-shaped, glinting with wonder like a child's. She was, he thought then and never had reason to change his mind, even more beautiful than she'd looked in the photograph.

They had a cup of coffee in the station café, old man Ravezzi complaining throughout about the thin, insipid drink, saying that it was 'made from watered down Camp Coffee, or something worse'. Frank hardly spoke to Gina. He let Mrs Ravezzi and Joe monopolise the conversation. But he kept his eyes on Gina and he listened closely to everything that she said. When she left Naples, some Italian soldiers had taunted an old Jewish man who was minding his own business in a corner of her compartment. They'd been delayed in Switzerland when an avalanche covered the tracks and they had to wait all night for it to be cleared away. She talked, too, of a bus journey across a snow-covered Paris from one station to another. She'd seen the Eiffel Tower, the Seine, the Louvre. But she couldn't believe she was actually seeing them for herself, with her own eyes; it was more like watching them in a newsreel. She'd been ill on the boat, she said, so ill she thought she'd never survive.

'I was exactly the same,' said Mrs Ravezzi. 'I remember it well. Mind you, I turned out to be a couple of months pregnant at the time. Which is not something you'd need to worry about.'

'Not yet, anyway,' said Joe, making her blush and dip her eyes and earning himself an elbow in the side from his wife.

They caught the coast train just after nine. Frank went with them as far as Paisley. He told Gina that he'd see her on Sunday. He waited on the platform and waved to her as the train drew away. She shyly, tentatively, waved back.

*

A few months later, on the Saturday, Frank was working late again. The radio was playing in the back shop and Frank, in his shirtsleeves, was seated at one of the front tables. He'd taken apart one of the mixers he used for milkshakes. The bushes on the electric motor had gone and he was replacing them. The insides of the motor were laid out neatly on an open newspaper. He'd just slotted the new bushes home when there was a knock at the door.

'It's open,' Frank said, without looking up. Even after the robbery, he still didn't lock the door. It was too much of a nuisance and, besides, the robbery was a one-off, he said. It wouldn't happen again.

After a moment, Frank looked up and saw a figure still waiting on the other side of the door, partially obscured by the 'CLOSED' sign.

'Come in,' he said, louder this time, thinking that whoever was out there hadn't heard him. But still the door didn't open. Frank laid down the casing of the motor and repeated, 'Just-a come in. Gie it a push.'

The handle turned and the door slowly opened.

It was Miller.

'Are you sure?' he said.

Frank took a moment.

'I'll just go,' Miller said, starting to turn away.

'No, on-a ye come. Please,' Frank said.

Miller leaned against the doorframe as he lifted his right leg over the doorstep. He let the door close behind him but didn't advance into the café. He stayed by the door, as if unconvinced that Frank had meant what he'd said. Miller was clean-shaven and generally more presentable than the last time Frank had seen him. There was nothing threatening about him, not in the least; Frank could see that instantly. But there was nothing particularly tentative or apologetic about him either. There was no hint of self-pity, none whatsoever. Frank said later that this was one of the things that drew him to Miller. It reinforced what he'd felt in court that morning, that sense of 'There but for the grace of God . . .'

'What do ye want?' Frank asked.

'Just to say thanks. For speakin' up for me,' he said.

Frank shrugged,

'It was a-nothin'.'

'I didnae understand what was happenin' in the court. But the policemen told me, as he took me down. He said I was lucky. I could easy have got six months wi' that judge, he said. He asked me why you did that. I said I didnae know.'

'I don't either,' said Frank eventually.

'Since I lost my job, an' things have no' been goin' so good, naebody's spoke up for me. Hardly a soul's put out a hand to me.'

Frank dropped his eyes, embarrassed.

'Well, anyway . . .' he said, and then let the sentence fade away. He turned and opened the door again. He was halfway out before Frank spoke.

'Where you-a goin'?'

'I've said what I wanted to say.'

'No, wait a minute,' said Frank, rising from the table at last. 'What are you goin' to do?'

The man was reluctant to answer but Frank had come to the door of the café now.

'I'll go tae Bute. I've still got family there, no one close. But I can probably find work an' somewhere tae stay.'

He nodded to Frank, starting to close the door behind him.

'Come back,' said Frank. 'Have a cup a tea.'

'It's better if I just go.'

'I was goin' to make somethin' anyway. Come on,' he said, holding out his hand. Frank remembered this moment, and this brief exchange, for the rest of his life. Was never able, really, to forget it. He would run it over and over in his mind's eye, like a piece of film on a loop. There was never any consoling ambiguity, never any doubt about the essentials; Miller wanted to go on his way into the night, Frank was the one who brought him back.

Miller sat at the table where Frank had been working and Frank made a pot of tea. Miller spoke guardedly about his month in prison. He'd tried to find a job afterwards but had no luck. So he'd decided to go back to Bute. He had little money and there was nowhere else he could go.

Frank thought about the idea of offering him a job before he actually did it; but there didn't seem, Frank said later, much to think about. Miller needed a job and, with the café getting busier day by day, Frank could use some steady help. Even now, when the subject was broached, it was Miller who was reluctant and Frank who was insistent. Eventually, Miller agreed to give it a try and said he would start in the morning.

People were surprised when they saw that Frank had taken on the man who had robbed him. But Frank said he was just someone down on his luck, someone who needed a helping hand. And soon people were accustomed to seeing Miller in the café. They pretty well forgot about the robbery or, at least, never mentioned it in front of Frank. Miller was a good help and he showed his gratitude to Frank in the best way possible: by never being late, never leaving early and generally doing everything that was asked of him. For the first couple of nights, he stayed in a cheap hostel at the back of the station. But Frank soon found him a room and kitchen in a tenement round the corner from the café. Miller knew nothing about running a café when he started but he was a quick and careful learner. When people asked about Miller, Frank would say that he'd sometimes had trouble with his staff, they would pilfer or take money from the till. But he'd never had any trouble like that with Miller. Frank had no worries about Miller, none at all.

Miller kept himself pretty much to himself when he was working in the café, even when it was busy. Frank was naturally gregarious; a social animal, keen to listen, keen to talk. But Miller stayed in the background and generally kept out of things. When people spoke to him, he was invariably polite but would say very little. He rarely engaged in any kind of extended conversation, even with the one or two female customers who made no great secret of their curiosity about him. Frank observed this, with some amusement, but never commented on it. That was Miller's business, no one else's. And besides, thought Frank, you always had to remember the leg; there was no knowing how something like that might make him feel about himself and about women.

✳

Soon, Frank was travelling down to Gourock every couple of days. He was closing the café early on Wednesdays so that he could spend the whole evening with Gina. There had been difficult spells in the first couple of months when Gina wanted to go home. She missed her sister too much, she said. She would never get used to this damp weather. She couldn't make any sense of the English or, as she said in her frustration, whatever language it was they spoke here. But all of this gradually passed.

When Frank first arrived, he'd spend fifteen or twenty minutes chatting dutifully with old man Ravezzi about how the café was doing. The old man took an inordinate amount of interest in all of this, having been effectively excluded from his own business by his sons. As soon as he decently could, Frank would say he fancied a bit of fresh air. And he and Gina would leave the house and cross the road to the prom.

On the prom, you're perched a few feet above the water, which constantly slaps and breaks against the sea wall. And you look out, like some tiny figure in a nineteenth-century landscape, at the restless glinting body of water hemmed in on the other side by mountains. It's the kind of setting which could induce a profound feeling of freedom and space but which could also, depending on your mood, remind you forcefully of your true significance, or lack of it, in the scale of things. The chances are, though, that Frank and Gina were too wrapped up in each other during their walks along the prom to dwell on any such thoughts.

The promenade at Gourock somehow became their own particular private place, like a room to which no one else had access. That was where they truly came to know each other. If the weather was even half-reasonable, they'd walk as far as the lighthouse and back again. If the weather was bad, they'd sit in a shelter, with the rain hammering on the roof as if it was trying to find a way in, their arms wrapped round each other. And they talked incessantly: about what they'd been doing since they'd last met, about Pozzuoli, about the people they knew, about what they might do in the future. In this way, during these quiet but pleasurable sessions, they became familiar with all the tiny inconsequential details of each other's life.

By April, Gina was working in the café for a day or two each week. Before long, she was there every day. And she and Frank decided that it would be sensible to take the next step. So they spoke to the priest and, with his help, arranged their wedding for the last Saturday in August.

Frank always remembered the night they went to see the priest. They had to see him quite late for one reason or another and Frank walked Gina to the station directly from the priest's house. To his surprise, Frank had been the nervous one. Gina had done most of the talking. The priest had spent several years in Rome and could speak Italian well, albeit with a thick Irish accent. Occasionally, Gina would turn to Frank, prompting him and telling him what to say. The priest had had his doubts, felt maybe it was too soon. But he was quickly won over by Gina's insistence and her charm.

While they were waiting on the platform at Gilmour Street, Gina was teasing him about how he'd been with the priest.

'Priests do that to me,' said Frank.

'Bad conscience,' said Gina as the train made its noisy arrival at the empty platform, seeming to protest at being made to stop.

'You haven't changed your mind, have you?' she said, teasing him, as Frank opened the compartment door.

'No!'

'Me neither,' she said, climbing in and pulling the door shut. As the guard blew his whistle, she pressed on the metal bar at the top of the window and slid it down. She beckoned Frank up to her. He jumped onto the step, feeling the train pull away under him, and kissed her. Or, rather, she kissed him. All of which surprised him as she never, normally, allowed any kissing in public.

He stayed there for a moment, the train picking up speed, the guard shouting at him. Then he dropped onto the platform, running with the train for the first few yards until he came to a halt. Gina was leaning from the window, smiling back at him. Suddenly, a cloud of steam swept down from the funnel of the engine and billowed along the side of the train like a grey sheet, obscuring her. For some reason, this agitated him. No matter how hard he tried, he could not see her. He even began to worry that something had happened to her. Absurd, he knew, but the feeling was very real. Suddenly, at the last moment, when her compartment was moving past the lights at the end of the platform, the steam lifted, snaking back into place above the carriage roofs, and he saw her – still leaning from the window, smiling, and waving to him – before the train swept her into the darkness.

2

It was a good summer, that year. There was very little rain and
there were long spells of just one glorious day after another.
During those weeks, people would say to Frank, 'Hey Frank,
does this no' mind you of Italy?'

'Aye-a so it does,' he would nod and, after a slight pause,
add, '. . . in the wintertime.' And he would hold back the smile
so that people weren't sure, at first, if he was being serious or
not. But, soon, both he and they would be laughing. No one
ever minded this teasing or the gentle but unswerving insistence
that Paisley wasn't Italy and never would be. That was just Frank
being Frank. No one would expect him to be any different. It
was understandable he should feel that way, only natural really.
And no one would have held it against him. The fact was, nobody
in the town ever had a bad word to say about him. That was the
thing about Frank: pretty much everybody liked him.

That summer, partly because of the good weather, the café
was doing better than ever. Gina was working there six days
a week, travelling up from Gourock in the morning and back
in the evening. The three of them – Frank, Gina and Miller –
quickly settled into their own routine. She stayed mostly in the

kitchen and the back shop, cooking and baking. Frank dealt with the bills and the money and generally supervised proceedings, like a ringmaster, from the counter. Sometimes he'd serve, but he usually had a couple of women to do that. Miller helped wherever he was needed, generally without prompting. He took care of the heavy lifting along with the cleaning and the washing and drying of the dishes and cutlery.

Miller and Gina were wary of each other at first. He worried that she would somehow displace him, render him unnecessary or perhaps simply dislike him. Miller enjoyed working for Frank and wanted to stay, didn't really know what he would do if he had to leave. On her side, the lurid tabloid version of Miller's story relayed by the Ravezzis, with a few imaginative flourishes added privately by Mrs Ravezzi, meant it was some time before Gina was comfortable even being alone in the same room with Miller. Gradually, though, as the days and weeks went on, they grew to accept each other. Each could see that the other worked hard. Also, Miller could not fail to see what Gina meant to Frank. And that counted for a great deal with Miller. Frank had been more than generous to him so anything that made Frank happy was fine by him. After her initial cautiousness, which Miller could well understand, Gina treated him just as Frank did. She neither assumed airs nor ordered him around. She didn't make him feel that he mattered any less, in the running of the place, than herself or Frank. The three of them seemed to be, as it were, equal partners.

In the early summer, Frank had the flat above the café decorated and refurnished. He paid cash in hand for the new furniture and the decorating. The business could afford it, he said, and Gina deserved it. He was keen to have everything shipshape and finished for the wedding. Which, of course, it was.

As the summer went on, there was more talk of war. No one was very sure what would happen. 'A' just hot air,' some folk would say. 'It'll no' come to anything. We've too much in common wi' the Germans for them to want to fight us.' But not everyone thought that. There were plenty of people who said quietly that the war would come sure as night. Frank tended to agree with them, but whenever anyone asked him, he liked to be hopeful and say it looked more like fifty-fifty. Mostly, that summer, he and Gina were too wrapped up in each other to bother very much about what was happening in the wider world. If the war did happen, they reasoned, they would worry about it then. For the time being, they would put it out of their minds and concentrate on the changes that were about to happen in their own small world.

✯

Frank opened the café as usual on the morning of the wedding. Most of the customers knew he was getting married that day and those that didn't soon found out. Many people looked into the café for no reason other than to wish Frank well. And many of them brought gifts or flowers for the young couple. That Saturday was a good day in the café, one that Frank remembered long afterwards and always with the greatest of pleasure. Perhaps, he sometimes wondered, that was because it had been the last good day, the last purely *good* day. But then he would quickly correct himself. That just wasn't true. That wasn't true at all.

At the café, everybody seemed to catch the mood and there were so many teas and coffees and cakes given away for nothing that Frank said it was probably the worst day's business in the café's history. Frank was teased rudely and relentlessly by both men and women. There were mistakes in the orders, much waiting around for food and ice creams and several times a tray of glasses or a couple of plated-up meals went crashing onto the tiles to a cheer and a round of applause. But nobody minded. And nobody complained.

There was a small crowd of customers, including Robert Glen, outside the café when Frank emerged, in his suit, for the wedding. Frank was all set to walk to the chapel. But Robert said they weren't having that and despatched a passing boy, who was given no choice in the matter, to the taxi rank. Miller appeared, in a suit of sorts, while they were waiting for the taxi. Some people were surprised that Frank had invited him but they supposed, when you thought about it, he couldn't really do anything else. After the first few moments, no one bothered much about Miller, which was often how it was. Miller tended to hover on the edge of things, generally unremarked; there, but never very directly or emphatically involved in what was happening.

There weren't many people at the chapel: Miller, the Ravezzis, three of their sons (one of whom acted as Frank's best man) and several other members of local Italian families. Some of the women who served in the café also turned up. Gina looked, as Frank remembered it, better than ever in her plain white dress. Most of the time, you didn't notice how good-looking she was because she didn't draw attention to herself. But there was no mistaking the fact that afternoon. None whatsoever. Frank could feel her shaking with nerves when she arrived beside him at the altar and, later, when they were married and the priest said that he could kiss her. She looked happy though, and she was glad to lean against him and relax a little for the first time that day. They went from the chapel in a convoy of cars down to Gourock where they had a meal in the Ravezzis' restaurant. The food was good and plentiful and there was more than enough to drink. Miller didn't drink at that time so he was even more to one side of things than usual. But that didn't bother him. He was apparently content to sit and listen to the singing, though he couldn't understand a word of it.

At eight o'clock, Frank and Gina took the last boat from Gourock to Dunoon. Some of the Ravezzis went with them and escorted them noisily to their hotel, a large mock-Tudor building almost opposite the slipway where the boat still docks to this day. After Frank and Gina had checked in, and the Ravezzis had sufficiently embarrassed them by making sure everyone in the hotel knew they were on their honeymoon, they were left alone for the first time that day.

They didn't make love that night. Gina was too tense, her body locked with nerves and exhaustion. But they made up for it the next morning and many more times during the course of the following two days.

✳

On the next Sunday, Frank and Gina went to early mass. People were pleased to see them and those who hadn't met them since the wedding offered their congratulations. There were a few teasing jokes about 'newly married' life that brought a blush to Gina's cheeks. And there was some quieter tight-lipped talk about the war. For months, it had been a shadow in the background. Now the shadow was closer, darkening things around them, no longer easy to ignore or dismiss. On the way back from chapel, Frank told Gina that they had no need to worry about it. The war wouldn't affect them. They would keep their heads down, work hard and hope, like everyone else, that it would be over soon. Then he changed the subject, reminding her, with a grin, of what someone had said about the glow in her cheeks.

'That was nonsense,' she said, the colour flooding even more vividly into her face.

'No,' said Frank, stopping and studying, as if to check. 'It's perfectly true. And I know exactly why it's there. It's because of last night, that time when you –'

Gina walloped him on the shoulder and gave him an earful, in Italian, of course, which was what they always used when they were together. And it only made Frank smile all the more, which in turn only made her tear into him even more. But after this, while they were making their way up Causeyside Street, she held his arm tightly. Both of them deeply happy.

At eleven o'clock that morning, Frank and Gina were in the front room of the flat above the café when the news came through on the radio that war had been declared. Frank was standing on a chair, holding a length of curtain material up to the window so that Gina could judge where to put the hem. Neither of them spoke for a moment or so. Frank stepped down from the chair and put his arms round her.

'We'll be okay,' said Frank.

She nodded,

'I know.'

They kissed and she moved away from him, telling him that she was fine and not to fuss.

Outside, the sky was still clear blue. The walls of the offices and warehouses opposite, empty because it was a Sunday, were washed with a warm autumn glow. The street outside the flat was quiet, just the odd car rumbling over the cobbles as it passed into Causeyside Street. There was an almost dream-like stillness in the air. Then, after a few moments, the pavements began to fill with people. They were moving this way and that, abruptly stopping and retracing their steps, suddenly crossing the road if they saw a familiar face. They would stop for brief bursts of conversation, people talking over each other, nobody really listening to anyone else. Then they would move quickly on, still chattering animatedly. Frank went downstairs and stood at the open door of the café, snatching a word here and there with folk who passed. They were frightened, he could see that. But they were also excited, exhilarated, lifted for the time being out of the boring ordinary. Gina came down and sat behind him at a table near the door. She had the curtain material folded in her lap but she didn't do any sewing, couldn't take her eyes off the people outside.

Around twelve thirty, air raid sirens sounded somewhere far off, maybe in Glasgow, maybe Clydebank. People started running and looking up into the sky. But after a time, the sirens fell silent again. Soon after this, Miller arrived at the café.

'You all right?' he said.

'Fine,' said Frank. 'Why should we no' be?'

'Just checkin',' said Miller. 'You mind if I stay for a while?'

'I'll make something to eat,' said Gina. 'Might as well keep myself busy, eh?'

When she went into the kitchen, Miller told Frank that there had been some trouble. There was only one German family in the town, living up in Oakshaw, the father a teacher in the John Neilson. They'd had a window smashed. And there was talk about having a go at some of the Italian families, too. So far, though, it hadn't been anything more than talk.

'Why-a should they have a go at us. Italy's no' at war with anybody. No' yet anyway.'

'You know what folk are like.'

'We'll be okay here,' said Frank. 'Nobody's a-goin' to hurt us.'

'You're probably right. But I'll wait a while even so.'

'Suit yourself,' said Frank. He thought it was unnecessary for Miller to stay with them. But he was grateful for his thoughtfulness.

Things calmed down again later in the afternoon. There was even a note of disappointment, a sense of letdown. And it was much the same over the next few days and weeks as people went back about their daily business, slipping reluctantly into the same old routine. Nothing really had changed. Not yet anyway.

✳

The trouble started a month or so later. Even then, Frank didn't get the worst of it.

Things were shouted at Italians in the street. They were pushed and jostled, but nothing more serious than that. In one of the cafés, there was a fight when a soldier refused to pay his bill because he 'wasnae handin' money over tae an Eytie.' Robert Glen dealt with this and told Frank that the soldier was half-cut, hardly knew what he was doing. When Robert got him back to the cells, he gave him a kick up the backside and kept him in overnight for good measure. Robert wasn't having any of that nonsense in this town, he said. But, even so, he told Frank to be careful.

'People are frightened,' he said. 'An' you never know what folk'll dae when they're frightened.'

He told Frank about the woman with the daschund. She was coming down News Street when a bunch of neds surrounded her and told her, 'That German dug needs pittin' doon.' 'Nonsense,' she told them, 'this dug wis born in Paisley. And its mother wis born in Paisley, tae. It's probably mair Scottish than a' you pit thegether. Now get oot ma way or I'll gie ye whit fur.' And when they tried to grab the dog, she laid into them with her handbag. 'The dug barkin' its heid aff an takin' a snap at any arms, legs or hauns in gnashin' range.' She soon scattered them like confetti to a general round of applause from the assembled onlookers and bystanders. He doubted if she, or the daschund, would have any more trouble, and even if she did, 'She's no' gonnae need any help from me.'

'In fact,' Robert said, 'if I get her name, I might even see if she fancies a job.'

*

In the second week of October, someone broke a window at the front of the café. Next morning, while Frank, Gina and Miller were still clearing up, the shopkeepers and pub-owners roundabout took up a collection for Frank. This raised more than enough to cover the cost of the new window. Frank was touched when they gave him the money and insisted that he accept it, despite his protestations that it was 'just-a one of those things, no' worth botherin' about.' Whenever Gina worried about what would happen to them over the next few months, Frank would remind her of this and say, 'That's the kind of people you're dealing with. I tell you – we're going to be okay here.'

In December, when Italy was siding more openly with Germany and withdrew from the League of Nations, there were yet more disturbances in the town. One Italian café was attacked by a mob, mostly drunk, on a Friday night. They tried to burn it down but the police and fire brigade were there before any great damage was done. Frank had no real problems in The Bay but he was aware of a shift in people's attitudes. It wasn't particularly to do with the fact that he was Italian. It was something more profound and far-reaching than that. People were realising that the war wasn't going to be over in weeks; it was a more serious, much more real undertaking than it had seemed at first. There was an uncertainty about things now. The future was no longer settled, no longer easy to make assumptions about. No one could view it now as merely an unbroken extension of the present, more of the same. The future had become dangerous and unpredictable.

In the café, they were still as busy as ever. They would see the occasional man in uniform. Some things – like coffee and corned beef – were harder to find from suppliers. But that was about the extent of how life had changed, to all intents and appearances, anyway. Frank concentrated his energies on running the business and tried to put the war to the back of his mind. By this time, Gina was pregnant and that helped to distract them, draw them even further into their own private world. Those months before and after Christmas 1939, Frank always said, were the happiest of his life. Aye, he would sometimes add, he and Gina were happy then, maybe too happy for it to last.

★

In January 1940, Frank noticed business was dropping away. There was nothing sudden or drastic about this. But there was no doubt that they were quieter. The café was completely empty at certain times now and there were no longer queues out of the door on Friday and Saturday nights. He was scaling back on orders for bread, meat and vegetables. And he laid off two of the waitresses. He was almost apologetic when he told them he was letting them go. He said he was very sorry, had no choice, and as soon as business picked up he'd have them back again. Even so, one of them turned on him angrily and said, 'What could ye expect from one of your kind, anyway?'

The other families, like the Ravezzis in Gourock, were having much the same problems. Old man Ravezzi told him about the Fareses in Glasgow who had thrown out all the pictures of Italy and gone through the menu stripping out anything that sounded even remotely Italian. They'd changed the café's name from Farese's to The Caledonian Tea Rooms. After this, business picked up a little, or so people said, but Frank had no inclination to follow suit. It was dishonest, he felt, almost cowardly. And it didn't really change anything. As Frank said, even if he turned the café into Granny's Heilan Hame, he and Gina would still be there. And they would still be Italian. No one could ever alter that.

There was no more trouble in the café, not then anyway. The days passed quietly for the most part and there were still enough customers to keep them turning over. Gina was showing now and people were genuinely delighted when they guessed or had their suspicions confirmed. It was clear to Frank that there were some customers whom they'd never lose; the others, well, there was nothing he could do about them so why worry? Miller had tried to join the army but had been rejected because of his leg. He continued to work at the café every day, being there pretty much from first thing in the morning to last thing at night. Frank told him he should take time off now and again but Miller said he didn't mind. He preferred to be working. He was now helping Gina with her English and he gradually took over some of the preparation of the vegetables. On the whole, Frank found himself withdrawing more and more into his work in the café and his life with Gina. He focussed on her warm taut belly and forgot about the wider world. He was still convinced they'd get through by keeping their heads down and working hard. That was all they had to do. All they could do.

✶

One night, at the beginning of March, Frank found himself suddenly awake. It was still completely dark so it must be two, three o'clock at the most, he thought. It couldn't be any later. He felt for Gina beside him, though he somehow knew already that she wasn't there. And then he registered the sound that had wakened him: a stifled sobbing from the hall.

'Gina! What's wrong?'

He was out of the bed and in the hall almost before he'd finished saying the words. He switched on the light. Gina was leaning against the doorway of the toilet, clutching her stomach with one hand, holding the other between her legs. Tears were running down her cheeks. And she was shaking her head.

'I'm bleeding.'

Frank dragged a chair from the kitchen and eased her gently onto it. He ran downstairs and picked up the phone, pressing the receiver over and over until the operator answered. As soon as he'd called the ambulance, he went back upstairs. He pulled blankets from the bed and wrapped them around her. He dressed quickly, hands fumbling with the buttons of his trousers and the laces of his shoes. He knelt beside her, putting his arms round her, and told her that he needed to take her downstairs. He lifted her up, holding her like a child. She pressed her head into his chest and he could feel spasms of pain lurching through her body. He carried her downstairs and, still holding her, unlocked the front door of the café. Then he sat at one of the tables, Gina still in his arms, and waited for the ambulance.

The ambulance-men asked him to lay her on the stretcher. Frank put her down gently, removing the blankets as he did so. When he stood up, he could see that the blankets were dark with blood. And he noticed one of the ambulance men glance at this and quickly look away again, saying nothing. Frank dropped the blankets on the ground and followed them. Frank wasn't going to lock the café but the ambulance man who'd seen the blood on the blankets insisted, said it would be better. He did as he was told, barely thinking for himself now. There were still some lights on but he wasn't going to worry about that. He climbed into the ambulance and took Gina's hand. She looked paler than he'd ever seen her. And her eyes were drifting away from him, dark pools of pain.

At the hospital, they took Gina away from him and told him to wait in the corridor. A nurse brought him a cup of tea but said she couldn't tell him anything; she didn't know how his wife was doing. Eventually, just before seven, when the sky was becoming a thin cold grey, a doctor came and told him that Gina had lost the baby.

'How is she?'

The doctor tilted his head slightly to one side.

'Lost a lot of blood,' he said.

'Can I see her?'

The doctor was reluctant, about to say no.

'Please,' said Frank. 'I-a have to see her.'

'For a moment. That's all.'

The smell of antiseptic almost made him gag. Gina was on a table in the middle of the room, covered with sheets that were streaked and dappled with blood. Frank thought at first that she was dead but was quickly reassured by the warmth of her hand. And he saw her move, too, just very slightly turn her head towards him, though her eyes remained closed. All around him, nurses and doctors were cleaning instruments or attending to their various tasks at trolleys and tables. It was as if some kind of performance had been briefly suspended while he was here but would start again as soon as he left.

'She's got a long way to go,' said the doctor.

'Will she be okay?'

'We hope so,' he said. Then he ushered Frank back out, arm on his shoulder, reminding him that they'd agreed on just 'a moment'.

Ian Miller turned up soon after this. He'd heard from the people who lived above the pub on the corner about the ambulance. He sat on the bench beside Frank and said how sorry he was, genuinely sorry. Frank nodded and told him what had happened, going over it detail by detail, as if by closely examining the sequence of events he might still discover some way of changing things.

'What d'you want me to do about the café?' said Miller.

'Forget the café.'

Then he added, after a moment,

'Don't worry – I'll pay you.'

'I just meant – d'you want me to open it? I can manage, more or less.'

Frank shrugged, his mind still in the operating theatre with Gina's frail punished body.

'Sure, if a-you want.'

Frank didn't move.

'I'd need the keys, Frank,' Miller said.

Frank handed them over.

'Ye sure about this?' Miller asked.

'Aye,' Frank said. And he nodded, not really thinking about the café or the keys or Miller. None of it mattered. Nothing mattered but Gina.

'I'll check wi' you later,' Miller said. 'If there's anything you need, just phone us, eh?'

'Aye, sure.'

Miller waited with Frank for another ten minutes or so then returned to the café. One of the barmen from the pub came up to lend a hand. And he sent messages to the women who still worked part-time at the café, asking them to come in. They didn't do much in the way of meals that first day but they kept the café open until evening and did reasonable business all considered.

At the hospital, Gina had been moved into an isolation room. She'd developed a fever and, as the doctors had feared, toxaemia. At the end of that first day, around ten o'clock at night, a young woman doctor nervously told him that Gina might not survive till the morning. They allowed Frank to see her. But again it was only for moments. She looked worse, her skin a kind of waxy parchment, dull and lifeless. She shivered occasionally and didn't respond to him. Miller came to the hospital again later with food but Frank couldn't touch it. He stayed on the bench in the corridor all night, waiting, fearing that they would come for him. But they never did. Time and time again, a nurse or a doctor came along the corridor towards him and he thought that they were coming to tell him she was dead. But mostly they kept walking and the few who stopped would only ask if he was okay or wonder if he needed anything. Gina survived the night though the doctors warned him against being hopeful. She was still very ill, the poison raging in her blood.

This went on for the next three days. Miller opened and ran the café as well as he could while Frank stayed at the hospital. Eventually, Gina's fever broke and the doctors became more hopeful. Frank went back to the flat that night for the first time. He took no interest in what was happening in the café, simply went up to bed and slept. In the morning, he returned to the hospital. And Miller opened the café again, as before.

It was almost two weeks before Gina was out of danger completely. During that time, Frank hardly set foot in the café. When they moved her to a convalescent home in Barrhead, Frank finally came into the café one night as Miller was locking up. He sat at a table and told Miller the good news: Gina was going to be okay but would need to rest. There was still a chance, too, that she could have another baby but they weren't even going to think about that yet. Miller handed Frank a metal tin which contained all of the money he'd taken in the café over the last couple of weeks. He'd paid, and accounted for, the milk and the bread and the other deliveries. But everything else was there. Frank looked at the money in the tin for a long moment.

'I don't know what to say.'

'Don't say anythin'.'

Miller placed the keys to the café on the table, beside the tin, and left.

*

It was a while before Frank was back in The Bay full time. While Gina was in the convalescent home, he could only see her during visiting hours: three to four and seven to eight every day, except Sundays when there was no evening visiting. It was the best part of an hour on the tram and bus to the home in Barrhead. But Frank was there at every opportunity. He was waiting outside the ward doors before they were opened and was generally last to be hustled out by the nurses long after they'd rung the bell. So for weeks, even after Gina was out of all danger, Frank was rarely in the café after lunchtime. Miller kept the place ticking over, though of course people missed Frank. Frank had such a comfortable, easy way about him. He was warm, expansive, genuinely interested in other people, always ready for a talk or a laugh, a smile never far from his lips. None of this, of course, applied to Miller though everyone accepted he was doing his best in the circumstances.

After Gina came home, things gradually returned to normal. Frank was in the café most of the time and he would nip upstairs to check on Gina regularly throughout the day. With Frank back in charge, Miller slipped naturally out of sight again, at least as far as the customers were concerned. Frank asked if he wouldn't like to stay in the front shop or do some of the cooking, which he could clearly manage. He said he wasn't bothered, was happy to do what he'd always done. Miller had enjoyed his time running the café. There was no doubt it had given him a certain satisfaction. And he liked the fact that people looked at him slightly differently since he'd been running the café, somehow took more notice of him. But all of that was of no great importance, it seemed. He was simply pleased to have Frank and Gina back; pleased, too, that he'd had the opportunity to repay Frank.

When she was stronger, Gina came down to help them for an hour or two each day. She was still frail, the skin under her eyes so dark it looked bruised. People in the café would go quiet and say under their breath, 'There's Gina down.' And they would shake their heads, wondering if it hadn't all been too much for her. Fairly soon, though, Gina was working a full day again and each of them had reverted to their usual roles as if nothing had ever happened to disrupt the smooth running of the business.

During this period, Frank and Miller had long relaxed conversations as they cleaned up after the café closed for the night. Sometimes, Frank would tell Miller about Italy and what it had been like living in Pozzuoli. Sometimes he would talk about Gina and how scared he'd been at the prospect of losing her. Miller gradually became more forthcoming about himself. He was still guarded and cautious with everyone else, Gina included, but he seemed to trust Frank without reservation now. Frank learned that Miller's mother had died soon after he was born so he'd never known her. He'd been brought up by his father and his sister, mostly his sister. She'd been thirteen years older than him. His father was dead now, his sister too. She'd married late in life but the man had turned out to be a waster who beat her. Once, Miller had given him a thrashing, fighting him in the backyard of their tenement in Rothesay. He'd moved to the mainland when his sister died.

It was during these conversations that Frank learned there had been a woman in Miller's life when he lived in Gourock. He wouldn't say much about this. But something had clearly gone wrong. She'd turned on him one night and told him, he said, what she really thought about him. Frank asked what he meant by this. But Miller wouldn't say any more, shook his head, closing the subject off to further conversation. Frank guessed, in her anger, she'd made some reference to his limp. He asked Miller why he hadn't met anyone since he'd been working in the café.

'I'm no' interested,' said Miller.

'Come on, you-a must be,' said Frank, grinning. 'I can think of one or two women that come in here who'd be keen if you-a gied them half a chance.'

'I know what women think of me.'

Frank was shocked by this reply.

'Ye're wrong,' Frank said.

'I know what I'm talkin' about.'

His lips were pressed tightly together; closed, like his mind, to the subject. He wouldn't meet Frank's eyes or Frank's sceptical, doubting smile. He was immoveable on this, rock-like. Frank felt that if he pushed any further, Miller would take it as a kind of insult. His cold, steely certainty wouldn't allow him to see it any other way. There was no negotiating, no possibility of compromise.

Frank shook his head, still gently insisting on his right to see things differently, and told Miller about a man back in Pozzuoli. This man had been caught in a house fire as a child. The side of his face was scarred and discoloured. He'd lost a hand in the fire, too. He'd never married, Frank said. He'd never needed to because he always had at least a couple of women on the go at any one time. He'd a good job as a guard with the railway company. People said he had women all over Italy. Frank didn't know about that but he certainly did well enough in Pozzuoli alone. The thing was – he never paid any attention to the mark on his face and his missing hand, none at all. He didn't think about these things so, in a way, it was as if he was just like any one else. And because that was how he thought, that was how the women thought, too. Frank grinned as he told Miller this story But Miller said nothing and went on with his work, mopping the tiled floor behind the counter. It seemed to Frank that Miller hadn't heard a word he'd said, hadn't wanted to hear. So Frank let the subject drop.

At night, when they lay in bed together, Frank would tell Gina about these conversations. She wasn't surprised to hear what Frank said. She'd always thought Miller was the one who cut himself off, who put up barriers. It was almost as if he was punishing himself, though for what reason she couldn't imagine. Such a pity, she would say, so wasteful and unnecessary.

Still, as they reminded themselves, warm in each other's arms, none of this was their concern. All that mattered was that he was a good worker and a good help in the café. There was, too, everything he'd done over the last few months. They didn't know what would have happened to the café if it hadn't been for Miller. Frank had tried to give him extra money, a bonus of a kind, but he wouldn't accept it; had insisted it wasn't necessary. So, while nothing really changed on the surface, Gina's miscarriage bound the three of them together even more closely. Miller still wouldn't talk to Gina overmuch. But she felt more comfortable around him; she'd lost the slight, residual wariness that she'd always felt in his presence.

✳

It was around this time, May 1940, that the war finally became a reality for most people. Until then, it had been a distant, even slightly disappointing affair. But all of that changed with Dunkirk.

This brought the war home to everybody. Suddenly, the war and the Germans were on the doorstep. The threat was obvious, the sense of danger impossible to ignore. People went about their usual business – or tried their best anyway. Frank had another window smashed by schoolboys and the takings continued to drop away week after week. It was clear that some people, even good customers, simply didn't feel right about coming into the café. This became obvious, beyond any shadow of a doubt, after Italy entered the war in June.

Frank and Gina had anticipated this for some time but it still came as a shock. As far as they were concerned, it was Mussolini and the *Fascisti* who'd declared war on Britain, not Italy and the Italians; but this distinction was lost on most people. When it happened, Frank decided to shut the café for a few days. He told Miller that he'd keep him on, if that was what he wanted. On the other hand, he and Gina would understand if Miller wanted to move on.

'No, I don't want to go anywhere,' he said. 'I want to stay here and see this through. Where else would I go, anyway?'

Frank smiled, touched by the sincerity with which he said this.

'Fine. If you're-a sure.'

'I'm no' leavin' now. No' as long as you can use me.'

'Good,' said Frank. 'Thanks.'

Shortly after this conversation, Frank was standing in the doorway of the kitchen, looking out at the empty café. Miller was scrubbing a copper cooking pan in the sink behind him. It was dark and there were no streetlights outside. In here, they had a light in the kitchen but it was well shaded. The rain was rattling against the windows and the few cars that passed hissed noisily through the water that was running down the street. Frank shivered, as if someone had walked over his grave.

'I think we'll-a need to get rid of this.'

'The pictures?'

'Aye. And maybe change the name, too.'

'Aye, maybe that'd be for the best,' said Miller after a long moment. 'I'm sorry.'

'I laughed at the people who did this earlier. Thought they were bein' daft. Nae bottle.'

'I don't see you have any choice, Frank.'

'I know.'

'You want me to help?'

'No. I'm no' a-doin' it now. But maybe before we open again.'

'Aye, whenever you like.'

'Maybe I'll get mysel a kilt,' Frank said, grinning. 'Think I've got the legs for it.'

'I dare say.'

'An you'll need tae gie me elocution lessons. Help me speak wi' a better Paisley accent.'

'Some folk would say that was a contradiction in terms.'

'Aye, maybe,' Frank said.

They were both smiling now.

'I think I'll go upstairs and see Gina,' Frank said. 'Just leave that pan to soak. Finish it in the mornin'.'

'You sure?'

'Aye, no' exactly any rush, is there?'

Frank locked up and went upstairs. Gina was in bed but awake, waiting for him. He changed and eased into bed beside her, pulling her to him. They held each other for several minutes, neither talking.

'What'll happen to us, Frank?' she said, in Italian as always.

'We'll be fine,' Frank said, holding her even more tightly. 'Just you wait and see.'

✶

Among the people whom Frank knew personally, the Ravezzi boys were the first to be interned. Several policemen arrived at the café, which like The Bay of Naples had not re-opened since Italy came into the war, and took the two younger sons. Another contingent went to Fabio's house to arrest him. Fabio refused to go quietly. Three policemen wrestled him to the floor in the front room with his wife and children watching, crying and screaming. The police used no more force than was necessary. Even Fabio admitted this later and said he'd have been better to do what they asked.

Most folk couldn't have been nicer, Frank said. They were sympathetic to the situation and concerned for him and Gina. They were on his side, he felt, even more strongly than they had been before. One day, he was up a ladder painting out the name of the café. He hadn't decided on a new name. But it was time, he thought, to get rid of The Bay of Naples. Miller was steadying the ladder at the bottom. Two boys passing on the other side of the street threw stones at Frank. One stone caught him on the cheek, cutting him. The woman who owned Polly Brown's, the sweet shop, grabbed one of the boys as he ran past her.

'Will I get the polis to him, Frank? I can hold this toerag while somebody fetches them,' she said, clipping the boy across the ear several times.

'No, let-a him go, Agnes.'

'Frank, he could've put your eye out,' said Miller from the bottom of the ladder.

'Let-a him go,' Frank said.

Agnes clouted the boy once more for good measure and released him. When he'd scurried away to a safe distance, he shouted back 'Italian bastard' and vanished round the corner with his friend. Frank shrugged and resumed the task in hand, laying the paint on thick and going over each letter several times.

Robert Glen was still coming into the café most days. At first, when the arrests started, he told Frank not to worry.

'I'll look out for you, Frank,' he said. 'They don't know what they're doin', nae idea. They send down these lists of names. Often the names or the addresses or both are wrong. And if you query one name, they say they'll check and come back to you. An' that's the last you ever hear of it. So I'm pretty sure I can keep you out of it, especially after what you've been through wi' Gina.'

But as June went on, Robert became less confident about his ability to protect Frank. They were getting tighter on the paperwork, he told Frank. They were making fewer mistakes with the names that were coming through now. There were still ways and means of helping people but it was becoming more difficult. He told Frank about Gandalfi, a wealthy Italian from Glasgow, who gave money to the Chief Constable to have his son released after he'd been interned. The Chief Constable took the money, so people were saying anyway, but made a mistake with the name. It wasn't young Gandalfi who was released, it was someone else entirely. Unfortunately, by the time they discovered this, young Gandalfi had already been despatched to Australia with a shipload of other internees. And, when old man Gandalfi complained and made a fuss, the Chief Constable had him interned too. It was the easiest way to keep him quiet. Of course, the Chief Constable still had the money old man Gandalfi gave him. There was no way he was giving that back.

'Well, there's-a nae chance of me payin' anyone off,' said Frank. 'I don't have the money.'

'I know that, Frank,' Robert said.

They were silent for a moment or so. Then Robert said, 'Listen, Frank. It's no' much but it's the best I can do. If I have to arrest you, I'll gie you as much warnin' as I can.'

'That's-a good,' Frank said.

'Least that way you can tell Gina yourself.'

'Thanks, Robert.'

*

That night, Frank told Miller that he was pretty sure he would be interned soon. It was just a matter of days.

'Maybe you should hide, Frank. Take off.'

'That would-a only make things worse. Anyway, where-a would I hide wi' an accent like this?'

Miller smiled and said, 'Still an' a', it's no' fair. Anybody who knows you knows that. But maybe it'll no' happen.'

'Maybe. But if it does, I want to ask you a favour.'

'Sure, Frank.'

'Open this place. Get it running, you and Gina.'

'By ourselves?'

'Just-a while I'm away.'

Miller shook his head.

'It's only what you did when Gina was ill.'

'That was different. There was nothin' else I could do.'

'It's exactly the same. Business has been bad for months.

Keepin' the place closed the last week an' a half has just about finished me. I need-a the place open and earnin' again. Otherwise, Gina'll have nothin'.'

They were sitting at the table in the back shop. The radio was playing dance band music. Frank could see Miller's reluctance, was worried he would turn him down flat. Miller wouldn't look at him and kept his body turned away from Frank. Frank felt a sudden rush of fear. He needed Miller. Gina couldn't manage the café on her own. That much he knew.

'Please,' Frank said, leaning across the table towards Miller.

'I don't feel right about it.'

'How no'?'

'Don't know that I could do it.'

'Course ye could.'

Miller said nothing, still unwilling to accept this burden.

'I don't have any choice here,' said Frank. 'Please, Ian. Gina needs someone to help her. Ye have to help us.'

'Have you spoken to her?'

'I will.'

Miller took a moment.

'Well, if it's what you want. Both of you.'

'It's-a the only thing we can do.'

They sat in silence for a few moments. Frank relaxed for the first time that day since he'd spoken to Robert Glen.

'We'll need to get rid o' this,' Miller said, waving his hand across the wall of pictures above him. 'Will you be okay wi' that?'

Frank nodded, 'But let's-a no' start now. I don't want to upset Gina any more than necessary.'

'It'll make it easier to get folk back in,' Miller said.

'I know.'

Miller shook his head, as if he would still choose to decline Frank's offer if he had any other option.

'Thanks,' said Frank. And shook hands with him, sealing the contract.

★

Frank didn't say anything to Gina that night. He considered it but decided to wait, hoping to find the right moment.

Two nights later, Robert came into the café at the back of nine. He had a cup of tea with Frank and chatted to Gina who was down in the kitchen that evening, checking recipes. Miller was also around but he was in and out, tidying up in the back shop and sweeping out the yard. Robert made Gina laugh with a couple of his stories about the blackout, which Frank would translate into Italian for her. There was, of course, the one Frank had heard several times about the man who came home at night and got into bed beside his wife. It was only in the morning, when he woke, that he discovered he wasn't in his own house but the house next door. Frank wasn't sure, as with most of Robert's stories, how much truth there was in this, if any. But they cheered Gina up and that was the main thing.

It was only later, after Gina had gone upstairs, that Robert said, 'I'm sorry, Frank.'

'What d'you mean?' Frank said, still thinking about how Gina had laughed and how beautiful she looked.

'We had word through about you. I have to take you tomorrow mornin'. Will that be okay?'

Miller had come to the door of the kitchen and was standing there, with the brush in his hand. He felt sick inside, remembering his promise. He'd never thought this would happen, certainly not so quickly. He was sure Frank wouldn't be taken, that Robert Glen would find a way to keep him here.

'Aye,' said Frank eventually, breaking the silence. 'I'll be ready.'

That night Gina cried and struggled, lashing out at Frank, insisting she would go with him. She wouldn't stay here on her own. Why did they have to lock him away anyway? Frank wasn't a danger to anyone. Surely they could see that? Slowly Frank calmed her and told her what he'd agreed with Miller. It would be good for her to work, he said. It would keep her occupied. Besides, they needed money coming in again. Miller had helped them out before. He would do the same again. And when Frank came back, they would repay him handsomely. They would make sure of that. They wouldn't take no for an answer this time.

Gina fell asleep in Frank's arms early in the morning as the light started to leach into the sky. Frank lay on the bed with Gina, holding her, until the sun flared on the slates of the roofs opposite. He gently extricated himself, without waking her, and started packing a suitcase. He wasn't sure what to take, had no idea where he was going or how long he'd be gone. Eventually, he had the case packed and he took it downstairs and stood it beside the front door of the café.

He was ready and waiting when Robert arrived with a young constable. Gina held onto him, as if this was all it would take to keep him here, until Robert had to say, 'We need to go now, Gina. I'm sorry.'

Robert was a tough old policeman with short grey hair and the scars of many Friday and Saturday night battles. But his eyes were glistening as he eased Gina away from Frank. Robert was angry with himself, angry with the war, angry with the world. But none of that would make any difference. Frank shook hands with Miller, who'd been there since early morning, waiting to see him off. Then Frank picked up his suitcase and walked out the door of the café, Robert going first, the young constable following on behind. Frank glanced back into the café as he passed along the front windows. But none of the lights were on inside. So, while Gina and Miller could see him clearly, Frank couldn't see either of them. He couldn't make out anything at all in the blanked-out interior of the café.

3

Gina went upstairs after Frank left.

She believed – actually 'knew' in her heart – that Frank would be back almost immediately. They would realise they had made a mistake. It was foolish to be locking up someone like Frank. Or Robert Glen would, somehow, 'magic' Frank out of this. So she drew a chair over to the bedroom window and sat there, expecting to see Frank come hurrying across the road towards her. She was shivering slightly, tense with shock, her body way ahead of her mind in comprehending her situation.

After an hour or so, she crawled onto the bed, hiding her face from the light, as if this would change anything. By evening, as the sky darkened above the roofs of the offices opposite, she knew with a cold pure certainty that Frank was gone from her life, for now anyway.

＊

For long stretches throughout that day, Miller could hear her crying, sometimes howling like an animal. He wished that he could somehow make a difference. But he doubted that anything he could say or do would bring her comfort.

He remained in the café, tidying up and cleaning, though with no very clear purpose in mind. Mostly, he stayed in case she did come down and there *was* something he could do. For a time, he considered going upstairs. But he had only been in the flat once or twice and it felt wrong to go there with Frank not around. Besides, what would he say to her?

By seven o'clock, when she'd been quiet for some time and there was still no sign of her, he decided to go home. He thought of calling up to let her know. In the end, he slipped out, locking the door behind him, without a word.

★

Next morning, Miller arrived at the café just after eight o'clock, much later than usual. He was surprised to find the door open and the lights already on.

Gina was sitting at the small table in the kitchen, where Frank kept the radio. She was drinking a cup of tea. The oven door was lying open and the acrid smell of oven-cleaner caught in his nostrils.

'Sorry I'm late,' he said.

'It's-a fine.'

Miller wasn't sure what to do here. He hadn't expected anything like this.

'Are ye all right? Well, I mean, as well as ye could be . . .'

'I am sorry about yesterday.'

It was difficult for her, speaking only in English. She frequently paused, struggling to locate the right word. But she was determined to do her best here. She had always spoken in English to Miller but Frank had always been there to pick up the thread of her thought when her mind raced ahead of her English, which it did often.

'Don't apologise. It was perfectly understandable. Terrible business, this.'

She smiled up at him. His obvious awkwardness made his concern seem all the more heartfelt.

'Would you like a cup of tea?' she asked, rising and going to the sink for a clean cup and saucer.

'I don't know. I –'

Miller frowned, rubbing his chin with his index finger. This was somehow too intimate, too personal. And it put them on too much of an equal footing.

'Sit down, Ian. Have a cup of tea with me,' she said. She sounded out the words like she was laying out a line of pebbles which had to be placed carefully with the right spacing between each.

'It's-a just us now. Please.'

So he sat down and she brought the cup of tea over to him.

'Robert Glen came in earlier,' she said, sitting opposite him and topping up her own cup. 'Frank went off in a lorry last night. Robert doesn't know where he's gone. But he said that Frank was all right.'

'That's good. I'm sure he'll be back soon. Really sure.'

'I hope so. That's what Robert said.'

Gina took a moment here, thinking partly about Frank and where he might be but also about the task before her.

'Frank wanted the café open again,' she said eventually.

'I know.'

'He said you would-a help me.'

'Aye, sure.'

'I couldnae manage without you.'

Miller pursed his lips, as if he was about to take issue with this observation. They sat in silence for a few moments. Miller put two spoonfuls of sugar into his cup and stirred it for longer than was really necessary.

'We'd need tae change a few things,' he said. He, too, was speaking more carefully and slowly.

'You mean the pictures?'

'They need tae go.'

'I know.'

'An' the menu,' he added. 'It's daft but –'

'It's all right. We'll-a re-do it in English.'

'An' we need a new name.'

Gina drew a breath at this.

'Do you have any ideas?'

'What about you? I thought maybe you . . .'

She shook her head vigorously.

'I can't do that.'

'I thought maybe just Albert Street Restaurant.'

'Aye,' she said, closing her eyes. 'That'll-a do as well as anything.'

'When would ye like to start?'

'Today,' she said firmly. 'That's-a what Frank would do.'

They began by taking down the pictures. They stacked these in the back shop and then Miller carried them upstairs to the flat.

'Will I leave them just here inside the door?' he asked when he went up with the first batch.

'No. We'll-a put them right upstairs.'

'Aye, sure,' he said, moving tentatively into the hall with half a dozen or so pictures in his arms.

'I don't want to be lookin' at them all the time,' she said. 'I would . . . prefer them to be out of the way.'

Miller nodded, understanding how she felt. They went up to the next floor, which had previously been used for storage but now was where Frank and Gina had their bedroom. She climbed into the loft and he passed the pictures up to her. She laid them carefully across the rafters, in stacks of five or six, and covered them with newspaper, to keep the dust off. When Miller handed up the framed newspaper page about Frank winning the swimming competition he said, 'You sure you want this one up there, too?'

She held the picture up in front of her.

'He looks-a so pleased with himself. Like a wean.'

Miller smiled at the 'wean'.

'I'll take that one back down, eh?' he said after a moment.

'No,' she said, laying it on a pile of other pictures and covering it with newspaper. 'They can all stay here till Frank comes home.'

Back downstairs, in the café, they started to remove anything that hinted of Italy. There were a couple of small Italian flags at the top of the large mirror behind the counter. These went, as did the sign which Frank had painted himself and which said 'Genuine Italian Ice Cream Sold Here'. The word 'Italia' in gleaming silver metal was soldered onto the top of the coffee machine. Miller took a hammer and chisel to this and chipped it off without doing too much damage. They threw out all the old menus. Miller rewrote them, expunging all Italian references, and paid a secretary in one of the warehouses opposite to retype them. Even some of the plates and dishes had to go. There were a couple of long plates that Frank used to display cakes and scones in the glass cabinet at the front of the counter. One of these showed a view of the Bay of Naples. The other two showed country scenes, people dancing on one, children and animals playing on the other. There was nothing specifically Italian about them but it seemed safer to dispose of them. Gina felt like crying many times that morning. Every glass and plate and picture had been put there by Frank. They had been chosen by him, bought by him, sometimes made by him. And as each item was removed, to be stored or thrown away, it seemed to her that they were removing, piece by piece, every trace of Frank from the café. It was like having Frank taken away from her for a second time. But she pushed on through this, kept going with the matter in hand, which is what Frank would have wanted her to do.

When this was completed, they turned to the more mundane and less painful business of cleaning the café and generally preparing to re-open for business. Miller ordered in supplies, usually discussing with Gina what they would need before he placed the orders. There were one or two companies which wouldn't supply them but not many and Miller could always find someone else to take their place. He worked long and hard that day and the next. She was touched by his effort, by his clear desire to do everything as Frank would have done it. No one else would have helped them like this. No one else would have done all of this so selflessly.

By the third morning, when the sign-writer was up his ladder, stencilling in the new name, they were ready for business. Miller wedged the front door open and put the new menu cards in the window. Gina waited at the door of the kitchen, well back from the counter, to see what would happen. After ten minutes, two women came in and settled down for tea and cakes. Miller took their order and passed it to Gina with a smile as if to say, 'There, I told you it would be just the same as before'.

By lunchtime, when the sign-writer had finished, and he was standing, paint pot in hand, on the other side of the street admiring his handiwork and hoping the rain wouldn't come to anything, the café was fairly busy again, echoing with the familiar clatter that had always given Frank such pleasure. Miller did all of the waiting himself. It was exhausting but he liked being out front again. And it was only now that he realised just how much he had missed this.

To Gina, who stayed in the kitchen, cooking and plating up the orders, it felt in some ways just like any other day. She kept thinking that Frank had simply slipped out for an hour or so. That he would be back any minute now. And that he would come up behind her, as he'd done many times before, when she was working at the sink, slip his arm round her waist and kiss her.

✷

Frank spent the first day and night of his internment in Gilmour Street jail, barely half a mile from the café. Robert Glen had apologised, for the umpteenth time since they'd left the café, as he put Frank in the cell.

'It's all right, Robert,' Frank had said. 'Nothin' you can do.'

'Bloody stupid this,' Robert muttered, shutting the cell door quickly and keeping his head down to hide his anger and embarrassment. For the rest of his shift, Robert wondered if he shouldn't simply let Frank go and send back a report saying 'not found at this address'. Just before he clocked off, he lifted the key from its hook and weighed it in his hand like a rock. The other policemen would back him up, turn a blind eye. Everyone liked Frank and no one was happy about taking him away from Gina, especially with her losing the baby a while back. After a few moments, though, he replaced the key and quickly left the station, unwilling to chance it. It may not in the end have made much difference. Someone else could have arrested Frank again the next day or at any time during that nervous summer of 1940 and things could still have turned out the same way. But Robert never forgave himself for this and for thinking of himself, and what might happen to him if he was found out, when he should have been thinking about Frank and Gina.

Frank was in the cell on his own until the evening when they brought in an old Italian who'd been a schoolteacher in Renfrew. The old man, Guido Castelvecchi, had sandwiches neatly packed in a tin by his wife. He kept holding the tin even after he'd finished the sandwiches. Later, when the old man lay on one of the bunks, covered with a blanket that smelled of vomit, he began to cry. Frank tried to comfort him but the old man turned away. Frank stood at the cell window for a long time that night, looking across to the back of the theatre. If he pressed his face against the left-hand side of the window, he could just see the bridge and part of the town hall. He couldn't see the town hall clock but he could hear it chiming out the hours and the quarters. He knew that Gina would be hearing these chimes, too.

The soldiers came early the next morning. They were young and unsure what to expect from their charges. They had rifles and fixed bayonets. When one of them hurried Mr Castelvecchi along with a push, Frank said, 'Wait a minute. Gie him a chance. He's an old man.'

'Shut your face and move it,' the soldier said, holding the butt of the rifle up close to Frank's face.

'Okay, okay, we're movin,' Frank said and helped Mr

Castelvecchi into the lorry where they found another half dozen dazed and frightened internees.

When they left Paisley, they were shuttled around the country, sometimes in covered lorries, sometimes in trains with the windows blacked out. For two days, they stayed in the same siding near a coalmine in the North of England as if (which was the truth) no one knew what to do with them. The station signs had been removed or covered in many places so it was often impossible to say exactly where they were. Sometime in the second week, Frank's train arrived in York station. And he and the other internees were taken, by lorry, to a local football ground.

The internees were marched from the lorries into the area under the main stand. Frank stopped as he entered, shocked by what he saw. A line of metal fencing had been erected across this area, the kind of fencing you would use to contain animals. Inside this cage, there were over two hundred men. They were crowded together, some sitting on camp beds, others sitting or lying on the floor.

The new arrivals entered the pen (which was the only way Frank could think of it) at the far end, where there was a gap in the fencing. There was a sergeant at a desk who took their details: name, address, next of kin. Once that had been done, they and their cases were searched. The soldiers helped themselves to anything of value. This was done quite openly. There was no attempt to disguise or conceal what they were doing. The boy who went through Frank's case was barely twenty. He had a young, hard face. He was worked up, adrenalin rushing through his body. His eyes were gleaming, as if he was in a kind of fever, and spit was glistening at the corners of his mouth. He took nothing but a silver-plated picture frame which had a photograph of Gina on their wedding day.

'No, please, no' that,' said Frank.

The soldier swore at him

'Just-a gie me the picture then.'

The soldier pushed him back roughly and started going through the next case. Frank thought about making a fuss, appealing to the sergeant. But the sergeant had seen it all and said nothing. Frank picked up the things that had fallen from the case when the soldier had rifled through it. He put them back as neatly as he could and closed the case. The frame didn't matter. And the photograph? Well, he would take plenty more photos of Gina when this nonsense was sorted out. Which, he had no doubt, would be soon.

Holding the case in front of him, he moved into the caged area, stepping carefully between the beds and the bodies, looking for a space that he could claim for himself.

★

Business picked up pretty quickly when word got around that the café was open again and that the food and cakes were as good as ever.

A few people commented on the changes but most were too embarrassed to mention the new name or ask about the pictures. Those who did make some reference to the differences in the café were usually old customers who had been fond of Frank and who felt, like Gina, that something of him had gone from the place. But, even so, no one disputed the need for the place to change. You couldn't have a café called The Bay of Naples, not in Paisley, or anywhere else for that matter. That would have been asking for trouble. Anyone could have told you that.

Gina and Miller worked pretty well together. They didn't

argue and hardly ever differed over how the café should be run. It was usually clear to each of them what Gina should do and what he should do. And they both worked equally hard. That was obvious to anyone who ever set foot in the café at that time, even to sceptics like Robert Glen. Gina had worried how she would get Miller to do what she wanted, how she'd be able to order him around – a man, several years older than her. But she found very quickly that she didn't need to order him around. Miller generally knew what was needed and simply got on with it, just as he had when Frank was here. Now, of course, he was doing more than ever before. But this, too, seemed no imposition.

Before he left, Frank had gone over the accounts with Gina. He showed her how the books were kept, took her carefully through the business of cashing up at the end of the day. He tried to make sure she understood how to keep track of what they were buying in each day and what they had in the way of stock. But he hadn't done this as often or as well as he would have liked. Every time he'd taken her through the books, Gina became upset and Frank knew that she wasn't concentrating on what he was showing her. Even so, when they reopened the café, keeping the accounts didn't prove to be a problem. Miller knew how Frank cashed up, had done it all himself when Gina lost the baby. So, when they shut up shop at the end of that first day, he guided her easily through this. He watched as she counted the takings, suggesting how much Frank would keep back for next day's float, how much Frank would set aside to pay suppliers and how much he would bank. He showed her, too, how to enter the correct amounts in each column of the daybook. It was fairly simple anyway, those first few nights, as they hadn't taken much in the way of money. But Gina quickly grasped the basics of it. And, within a week or two, she was doing the books by herself.

Initially, Miller was simply pleased that the café was reopening and that he had his job back again. Like Gina, he thought Frank would be home soon and everything would then return to normal. In the meantime, he was glad to help out. He still hadn't forgotten how Frank had extended a hand when most people would have turned their backs. Throughout his life, Miller had been used to people turning their backs. Even on the few occasions when he'd allowed people to grow close to him, it had usually ended badly. He still remembered, would never forget, the way things had ended with the woman in Gourock; how she'd lashed out at him with her words, mocking him for the way he was, damaged goods. If anything, this had reinforced his determination to keep himself to himself. And his experiences with most people had only confirmed him in this view; though you could argue, of course, that his attitude merely reaped its own harvest. Frank, however, had been different; he had treated Miller decently, better really than Miller had any right to expect. Frank had changed his life. He owed Frank. And he was pleased to be in a position to repay him.

Robert Glen looked into the café most nights. He tried to find out where Frank was and what might happen to him. But he saw pretty quickly that no one really knew what was going on with the internees. He didn't tell Gina this, though. He kept things vague, always trying to sound positive without raising her hopes too much. Mostly, though, the reason Robert went to the café was to keep an eye on Miller. He didn't entirely trust Miller and he was concerned about how Gina would manage. As the weeks passed, and he saw how hard Miller was working, Robert changed his view. He would shake his head and admit to anyone who happened to be listening, 'I'm no' often wrong about folk,' he would say, 'but I was wrong about him.'

Throughout all of this, Gina was relentless in her efforts to find out what had happened to Frank. She tried the police, the authorities, the army, the church. But information about the internees was always scarce and sketchy. She wrote to Frank every few days, care of an army address in Glasgow that Robert Glen had given her. In these letters, she told Frank everything that had happened in the café: who'd been in, who'd been asking for him and generally how well they were managing, all considered. She told him, too, how much she missed him, though she didn't dwell on this, not wanting to upset him or add to his worries. She spent hours on these letters, writing them late at night after a long day in the café when she could barely keep her eyes open. Writing and sending these letters brought her some comfort. She knew that Frank would want to hear from her. And she felt that it would help him, wherever he was, to know what was going on in the café and that they were managing well without him.

✳

At the football ground, more internees continued to arrive day after day. The new arrivals clutched their cases and bags as if they were lifebelts; their only, precious, tenuous connection with the settled, normal world of their previous lives. Most of them had the same dazed expression, as though they'd just been in a road accident. Frank figured he had probably looked exactly like that when he arrived, too. There were usually a few in each batch who were still full of bravado. But this never lasted; the wind was quickly taken out of them by their first sight of the cage and the indifference, or worse, of the soldiers. With this constant flow of new arrivals, the area under the stand was soon as crowded and rank-smelling as a pen full of animals. Frank had found himself a spot well away from the toilets which he shared with another Italian, Carlo Goldini. Carlo was seventy-six years old. He had trouble walking and Frank had helped him when he arrived, weary and bewildered, almost on the point of collapse. From then on, they'd stayed together, keeping a little piece of territory to themselves, watching each other's belongings when they finally had to brave the toilets.

Carlo had been a carpenter in a small town called Merano near the Austrian border. He'd never been out of the valley in which Merano lay until last year. His children – a son and daughter who ran a B&B on the front in Blackpool – had begged him to come and visit. He'd put them off year after year until finally, last summer, he'd agreed to make the journey. He arrived in Blackpool on the Saturday and war was declared on the Sunday. He had stayed on in the hope that the war would soon be over and things would return to normal. After a couple of months, he no longer had the option to go home because it was almost impossible to travel across Europe. At the beginning of June, after Italy officially came into the war, Carlo's son and daughter were interned. The police weren't sure what to do with him initially because he wasn't on any of their lists. However, they had come back a few days later and arrested him, too – 'just to be on the safe side', the police sergeant had said, as if Carlo could surely see the sense of it. By this time, of course, his son and daughter had vanished, lost in the general chaos.

Carlo had emphysema. He blamed the emphysema on the

wood dust and shavings from the carpentry work and absolutely, vehemently, denied it could have anything to do with the malevolent little roll-ups that were never far from his lips.

'What do you put in those things, anyway?' Frank said one afternoon, speaking to him as always in Italian.

'Only the finest Virginian tobacco,' the old man said, grinning.

'Smells like old shoe leather to me,' said Frank.

'That, too,' said the old man. 'Want one?'

'No thanks,' said Frank.

'The English have a phrase for it, don't they?' said the old man. 'Separating the men from the boys, eh?' And he chuckled to himself contentedly for a few moments, until the chuckling turned into a coughing fit. When this was finally, painfully, over, he looked up at Frank, the damp roll-up still clamped between his black-stained fingers.

'No, like I say, nothing wrong with these,' he said, bringing the wet end of the tight little roll-up back to his lips with something approaching reverence.

After a few weeks, Frank and Carlo were moved to a disused cotton mill in a small village south of Preston. If anything, the mill was worse than the football stadium. The machinery and furniture had been stripped out long since and the building left to the elements. Every window was broken and the wind and rain sailed through what was left of the frames pretty much unobstructed. The internees were kept on the ground floor and water drained through the ceiling like a colander whenever it rained, which it did virtually every day, sometimes all day. The mill was set against the side of a valley so that even when the sun did shine, the light and warmth never made their way down there, as if permanently excluded by something in the lease. Most of the time, Frank felt, it was like being underwater. There were no beds apart from half a dozen straw mattresses that had been tossed onto the ground when they arrived. These were reserved, by agreement, for the weakest and the sickest. There were over four hundred men crowded into that dark, damp place. Frank always said, even years later, that he could still feel the coldness of that mill in his bones. It was something he was never able entirely to forget.

The soldiers were on the whole pretty good, allowing them into the yard and even playing football with them at times. But there was still a wariness on both sides and a profound uncertainty, among the internees, about what would ultimately happen to them.

In the third week of August, the Germans began to bomb Liverpool. Some nights, the sky was lit up like day. Carlo would sit beside Frank when the bombing raids were taking place, looking at the sky through the broken windows. Most of the time, all Frank could see of the old man was the end of his roll-up shaking in the darkness.

'Are you okay?' Frank would ask.

'Si,' the old man would say, almost snapping at Frank. 'Non preoccupari per me.' *'It's not my business.'*

The noise of the bombs wasn't loud. But each one had its own presence. Each deep 'crump' had its own beginning, middle and end; the sound rolled towards them, opening out like some poisonous flower before it closed in on itself again. Although they were twenty miles or more from Liverpool, there was no mistaking the scale of what was happening there. The old man was always bad on these nights. His breathing became loud and wheezy. He coughed painfully and often; thin watery coughs that lacked the force to clear anything. And he persisted with the roll-ups even when each drag sent him into another fit of coughing. He needed to feel the crumpled paper and tobacco between his fingers. He needed to draw the burning air down his throat and into his lungs, or what was left of them.

Frank tried to dissuade him from smoking but he refused. The roll-ups helped him, he said. And besides, he would add, he was fine, there was nothing the matter with him. Frank could only sit and watch the tip of the roll-up glow as the old man took a drag. It would be quite still at these moments, held in his lips. But as soon as he pulled it away from his lips, the glow would begin to fade, though never entirely. And it would dance furiously in the dark now that the old man was only holding it in his trembling, loose-skinned hand.

★

During that summer, Gina's world gradually but steadily contracted. She focussed increasingly on the café and excluded almost everything else. She hardly went out, except to the bank. But then, as she herself said, there was no pleasure in going anywhere without Frank. Her visits to the chapel became less frequent. She still went to early mass most Sundays but she was either too busy or too exhausted to go at any other time. Occasionally, she would meet one of the other Italians in the town or someone would drop into the café for a chat. But this was happening less and less. Most of the families had their own worries. They had lost husbands and sons, too. And they were also trying to cope as best they could.

The café similarly took over Miller's life. He worked harder that summer than he'd ever worked in his life. He didn't think twice about this, accepted it as merely the right thing to do. And when the café was busy and everything was going smoothly, which it did most of the time, he took a real sense of pleasure in being the one who kept it running and held it all together. At those times, everything revolved around him. He controlled it all, like the leader of a dance band. As the weeks passed, and there was no prospect of the situation changing anytime soon, Miller settled fully and comfortably into his new role. He felt right at the heart of things now, right in the centre of his own life. Possibly for the first time ever.

When he thought back over the last couple of months, he was pleased, and not a little surprised, that things had worked out so well with Gina. He had been wary of her at first, unsure how she would treat him or how he should treat her. Miller had always been acutely aware of Gina as a young and very attractive woman, the kind of woman who would normally not look twice at him.

As it turned out, though, they had quickly and easily defined the dynamics and parameters of a very effective partnership. This had happened without any great discussion. They'd simply pushed on with the business of running the café and everything else had followed from that. They were equals of a kind now, making decisions together and disagreeing on very little. They had learned, over these recent difficult months, to rely on each other and to trust each other. But then they'd had to do this. This was the only way they could run the café efficiently and well. And that's exactly what they were doing by late summer. The café was busy again, busier than it had been before. They were taking more money some days than they'd ever managed when Frank was there.

*

At the end of August, they were moved again. Lorries came for them in the late afternoon and they were driven into Liverpool.

Most of the internees were silent and apprehensive as they headed towards the docks and saw for themselves the damage done by the bombs. One or two became increasingly restless and agitated. They knew that other internees had been sent to Canada and Australia. And they knew about the *Arandora Star*, which had been taking over a thousand internees to Canada when it had been torpedoed with the loss of most of those on board. Frank had heard that Ferdinando Biagioni, whose family had a café in Paisley, had been on the ship. He hoped that Ferdinando had been one of those who'd survived or that maybe he hadn't been on the ship at all; there was so much rumour and gossip and misinformation among the internees that you couldn't really be sure of anything. But it turned out to be true about Ferdinando. His family had a plot at Hawkhead Cemetery and, after the war, they put his name and an enamel photograph of the young man on the side of the family gravestone. Later, much later, when Frank went regularly to the cemetery, he would pass this stone and would usually pause and look at the photograph, which reminded him in many ways of himself. The Biagioni stone and the photograph are still there, on the left as you go up the hill, twenty or thirty yards beyond the memorial to the children who died in the Glen Cinema fire.

Frank asked one of the soldiers where they were going. The soldier just laughed, not unkindly, and said, 'What makes you think we know? They don't tell us anything.' Frank had long since accepted that he wouldn't be going home anytime soon; not tomorrow or the day after or even next week. But this moved the prospect way into the hazy distance, where you couldn't even be sure that it was still a possibility. And the worst thing was, there was nothing he could do about this, no one to whom he could appeal. No way that he could affect, to even the slightest degree, what was happening to him.

It helped that he had the old man to worry about. Carlo's breathing was laboured and noisy. Frank had almost had to lift him, with the help of some other internees, into the lorry. As the journey had gone on, he'd withdrawn more and more into himself, barely responding to Frank's attempts to engage him in conversation. The only thing that brought him out of this was when a young boy, no more than eighteen, became increasingly agitated as they entered the docks. He stood up and started yelling at the soldiers. No one else could understand what he was saying but, after a few moments, Carlo looked up at the boy and then began speaking to him. The boy fell silent for a moment then leaned down towards Carlo, shouting even more loudly at him, becoming more distressed. Carlo tried to calm him but this brought on a fit of coughing and the boy turned again to the soldiers, who were telling him to sit down and shut up.

'What's he saying?' said Frank.

'He says he's not going on a ship. He doesn't care what they do to him.'

'Tell him to sit down. They'll hit him.'

'He won't listen. He thinks they're sending us to Germany or back to Europe.'

Suddenly, one of the soldiers punched the boy in the face. He crumpled onto the floor of the lorry, his nose bleeding. It took Frank and several of the other internees to keep him down there, the soldiers standing over them, pointing their rifles. Frank held up his hand,

'It's a' right.'

'It better be.'

'He's worried about where we're going.'

'Yeah, well, tell him – so are we. Cos wherever you're going, we're going, too.' Frank told Carlo to translate this for him. And when he heard this, the boy finally stopped struggling and relaxed a little.

The lorry finally stopped beside a cruise ship that was well past its best days. The boy shook his head and held back when he saw the ship. Carlo kept talking to him, forgetting his own problems, as they joined the queue that was filing onto the ship. They were sent down to the very lowest level, the crew's quarters. Frank, Carlo and the boy took one two-bunk cabin and blocked the door so that no one else could come in. Eventually, as it was getting dark, the ship cast off and began to make its way out to the open sea. Frank left the old man with the boy and went up onto the main deck. There were hundreds of internees here, soldiers watching them from the higher decks. He saw the coast of North Wales falling away, surprisingly flat, on the left-hand side of the ship.

After an hour or so, the bombing started in Liverpool again. And the old man and the boy came up to join him; already, it seemed, an inseparable couple. It was as if someone had cracked open a door to hell. The faces of the internees were lit up from time to time like those of a cinema audience. Hardly anyone spoke, as if they were indeed sitting in the stalls, lost in the story unfolding before them. After a time, the bombing stopped. There were no lights showing on the ship and the moon was hidden by thick cloud so the darkness closed in around them with a vengeance. All they could hear was the churning of the engines and the muted splashing of the waves as the bow of the ship sliced through them.

✳

In the morning, when Frank woke, he was surprised to find that the engines were silent and the ship was stationary.

He leaned down from his bunk and looked out of the porthole. They were in a large open harbour crowded with small, brightly painted fishing boats. On his right, there was a grassy headland that rose high above the ship. There was something about the lush, rain-fed grass that made him think of Scotland. The boy was awake, sitting at the foot of Carlo's bed. He wouldn't move from there until Carlo was awake. Frank left the cabin and pushed his way along the corridor until he reached the other side of the ship.

He stopped at the first cabin with an open door. Two internees were standing at the porthole. Italians, with Birmingham accents.

'Where are we?' said Frank.

One of them stepped away from the porthole to let him see. Frank was surprised to find himself looking at an attractive little holiday town with a great sweep of esplanade above a sandy beach. Most of the houses along the front were white but those scattered further up the hill were blue or pink or yellow. And there was green everywhere, trees and bushes poking up between the houses

'Anyone recognise it?' said Frank.

'Sure,' said the younger of the two men, who both seemed amused at something.

'Where is it?' Frank asked with a shrug when neither of them looked as if they were going to let him in on the secret.

'Douglas,' said the older man.

'On the Isle of Man,' said the younger.

'What's-a so funny?' said Frank.

The two men looked at each other and grinned again, still amused by the same private joke.

'It's where we went for our holidays last year,' said the younger man.

'And it looks,' added the older one, after a moment, 'like it's where we'll be having them this year, too.'

4

On the night of the sixth of September 1940, according to the *Paisley Express*, a man caused a breach of the peace in the café. The item, in the following day's paper, was barely six lines long. It didn't give the man's name, simply said that there had been a disturbance and a man had been arrested. He was taken briefly to Gilmour Street jail but no charges were preferred. It was a neutral, unremarkable little item, in bold type, just one of half a dozen in a narrow column running down the right-hand side of the second page. There was nothing in it that would catch or hold your eye. Most people would have skimmed over it or ignored it completely. But the fact is that what happened that night changed irrevocably the lives of Frank, Gina and Miller; though, of course, none of them knew it at the time.

The sixth of September was a Friday and had been a long and busy day in the café. At lunchtime, Gina and Miller had people queuing out onto the pavement for seats. They'd barely drawn breath when they had the usual Friday afternoon rush of women wanting tea and cakes after they'd done their shopping. As soon as the women had gone, the couples, getting started on their Friday night out, began arriving for fish suppers and high teas. It was, if you took away the few men in uniform, a curiously normal Friday, just like any of those before the war. At times, when she was lost in her work, it seemed to Gina exactly like those other Friday afternoons, so much so that she took for granted Frank's presence out in the main part of the café. She expected to hear his voice at any moment, or feel him brush past her as he hurried to the big freezer in the back shop for more ice cream. Then she would stop and look up from what she was doing when she heard Miller's voice or remembered yet again, for no particular reason, the brutal fact of Frank's absence. The pain never diminished. Nothing ever wearied it or weakened it. Nothing could dilute its power and malevolence. With the passage of time, she had grown used to the pain but only in the sense that she had come to recognise it, like an acquaintance or relative, and had become intimately familiar with it. She would try to ignore it and push on with her daily routine. But the pain was always there, part of her and part of her life, inescapable.

Gina and Miller were kept busy all that Friday. They had two waitresses to help at lunch and teatime. But for the rest of the time they handled everything else between them and they did so smoothly and efficiently. Their way of working was well established by now. During mealtimes, Gina stayed in the kitchen and did the cooking. Miller would make the teas and coffees, write up the bills and take the cash. The waitresses would serve, sometimes with Miller's help. When there was no cooking to be done, Gina came out to the counter and made the teas and coffees and took money. Miller would then move out in front of the counter, seating and serving, wiping and cleaning. And that was pretty much how the day had gone, a close cousin to all the other days that had gone before it.

By the back of eight that night, when the last half dozen customers were still dawdling over their cigarettes, Gina and Miller were exhausted and ready for a seat and a cup of tea in the back shop. They wouldn't be finished even after the customers had gone; there were still dishes to be washed, floors to be mopped, tables to be cleaned and laid for the morning, when of course it would all start over again. Gina was behind the counter, drying glasses with a linen cloth. Two of the tables already had their bills. She was just waiting for the last table to ask for theirs. Miller was out in the back yard, stacking the crates of empty lemonade bottles near the door, ready to load onto the Struthers' lorry in the morning. She could hear the heavy rattle of the glass in the wooden crates as he banged them down one on top of the other. That was when the door crashed open, banging back against the coat stand and sending it flying over one of the tables. The man was still standing out on the pavement. He had kicked the door open and the outline of his right shoe, wet and dirty, was stamped on the lower panel of the door. The other people in the café froze in their seats, heads turned to the door. This must have happened in seconds but it seemed to Gina that he stood in the doorway for several minutes before she recognised him. He used to come in with his wife and sometimes his son, who was in his twenties. His name was Blair – Bobby? John? He'd always liked Frank and Frank had liked him. They'd talked about football, swimming – anything and everything. And the boy had been a footballer; good too, if she remembered rightly. Blair had stopped coming to the café months ago, long before Frank was taken away. Gina hadn't seen him since then.

She saw now that he was drunk, swaying slightly. He was

pointing at her with his right hand as he stepped into the café, bumping against the door frame. Miller was still in the yard, clattering down another crate. Blair stopped and looked around. There was something changed about him. He was quite unlike the genial, quiet, smiling man she remembered.

'So you've changed it, eh? Ye think that makes a difference? Ye think that makes it okay?'

With a sudden vicious movement of his arm, he swept a pile of saucers from the top of the counter onto the floor. They went smashing onto the black and white tiles, shattering into a blizzard of fragments. Gina was moving back against the big mirror, shaking her head. She could see now that he was crying. His eyes were rimmed with red and his nose was running like a child's.

'My only son,' he said, speaking to Gina though she didn't understand what he meant. 'Twenty-one years old. That's a' he was. Just a boy. Barely started.'

He picked up a large jar of penny sweets from near the ice-cream cabinet. Gina went down, hands over her head, as he threw it. The big mirror shattered and came raining down around her. She was crying herself now, almost hysterical, the glass peppering her hands and arms with tiny cuts. She heard Blair howl. He was saying something over and over again, a name – Thomas. Then she felt someone move past her and, after a moment, she heard Miller's voice.

'John, John, what you doin'? I know what happened. I heard the boy died. An' I'm really sorry. But this'll no' help. This'll no' bring him back.'

He was talking as you might to a child, soothing and reassuring.

'My only wean,' Blair said slowly.

'I know, John. I know,' Miller said. 'But it's no' her fault. It's no' Frank's fault either. You know that, John, don't you?'

Blair was shaking his head as if refusing to accept this. But he was already backing away from the counter. The other men in the café, those who'd been sitting at tables, were finally moving towards him. Miller waved them back. Gina was standing up again, watching, dazed, as Miller brought the situation under control. He was unafraid, hadn't cared what might happen to him even when he first came through from the back yard. When he spoke to Blair, it was obvious that he meant every word he said. And Blair knew this.

He collapsed into one of the chairs, sobbing, spent. Miller limped over to stand beside him and put his arm on Blair's shoulders. Miller continued talking to him but she couldn't hear what he was saying. Gina looked at the fragments of her own reflection on the floor all around her. She had managed to back into a space, under the shelf, where the crates of lemonade were kept and which Miller had just emptied minutes earlier. This was why she was relatively unhurt, with some tiny but not deep cuts on her arms and hands. If she hadn't taken shelter there, she would have been much more badly injured. There were people at the door now, drawn from the street by the commotion. They were edging into the café, gawking, taking it all in. Someone must already have sent for the police because two of them arrived quickly, pushing through the spectators and ushering them back outside. It wasn't, as Gina had hoped at first, Robert Glen. It was two older men, one of whom she'd seen with Robert before. They spoke to Miller and Blair for a while though Blair hardly said anything in reply. One of the policemen came over to her, looking at the few shards of mirror that were still fixed to the wall.

'Are ye all right, Mrs Jaconelli?'

'I'm all right now,' she said.

'I'm sorry about this. Is there anything we can dae?'

'No, it's just a case of clearing it up. We can do that.'

'Mr Miller says you probably won't want to press charges. The man's son was on a submarine and he was killed by an Italian boat.'

The policeman, slightly embarrassed, lowered his eyes as he said this. And now she saw that Miller was watching her, to see what she would do and whether she would go against him.

'Ye huv every right to press charges, Mrs Jaconelli. What happened to his son is nothing tae dae wi' you. You don't deserve this.'

'No,' she said after a moment. 'We'll no' press charges.'

She knew this would be what Frank would want. It was exactly what he would have done in the same situation. But she was conscious, too, of not wanting to contradict or undermine Miller.

'Okay. If you're sure.'

'Aye. Quite sure.'

'We'll take him down the station, let him sober up a bit. But if he comes back—'

'I'm sure he'll no',' she said.

'No. Probably no'.'

The policeman nodded and began to turn away from her. Then he stopped and added, 'Thanks, Mrs Jaconelli. A lot of folk wouldnae be so understanding. I'll tell Robert Glen what's happened. He'll probably come an' see you himsel.'

'Thanks,' she said.

'An' we'll get a' these folk out for you.'

'That would be good.'

When the police and the last of the customers had gone, Miller locked the front door and came over to her. He looked down at the silvered glass that covered the floor and shook his head.

'We'll get that mended. First thing. We'll get it back just the way Frank had it.'

She nodded, finding herself trembling now.

'Thanks for goin' along wi' me and no' pressin' charges.'

'That's okay,' she said, her voice still faint.

'You remember the boy?' Miller asked.

'Aye, I do.'

'Used to come in fairly often. Before the war, anyway.'

There was an awkward moment of silence between them.

'You better check those cuts,' he said finally. 'Make sure there's no glass in them.'

She nodded.

'Come on through to the back shop. I'll make us a cup of tea.'

'What about this?' she asked, looking down at the glass.

'I'll clear it up later.'

She sat at the small table in the back shop. She was feeling cold now and reached for the cardigan that she kept on a hook behind the door. Miller busied himself getting the kettle on and the pot and cups and saucers ready. Gina picked three needles of glass from her arms. That was all she could see and she reminded herself, yet again, how lucky she'd been. The blood from her arms had seeped onto her white cotton blouse. But she would take that off later. She would destroy it, burn it. She would never wear it again.

They sat at the table together and drank their tea in silence. She was grateful for both his presence and his silence. When she had finished her tea, she stood up, trembling worse than ever now. For some reason, it was as if the impact of everything had only just hit her.

'I'm going upstairs,' she said, and she could hear her own words stuttering and breaking up like a voice on the radio. 'Thanks for –'

She stopped. The trembling was taking over her body. She could see her hands shaking in front of her and hear her teeth chattering.

Miller rose and came awkwardly towards her. After a moment's hesitation, he put his arms round her. She pushed her face into his shoulder, her own arms limp by her side. Miller held her tightly against him. He could feel every bone in her body and she seemed as fragile and small as a bird. He could feel her ribs under his fingers and her hips were pressed against his. Her breasts were flattened against his chest. Her long dark red hair touched his cheek. He could smell the faint scent of soap or perfume in her hair.

After a few minutes, she stopped crying and moved away from him. He allowed her to go, didn't try to restrain her for a second.

'I'm sorry,' she said.

'It's all right. Terrible thing.'

'I'll see you in the morning.'

She turned away and went upstairs. Miller waited for a good few moments in the back shop. Then he started clearing away the teapot and the cups and saucers. He spent another hour or so in the café, sweeping up the remnants of the mirror from the floor and taking down the pieces of mirror that were still screwed to the wall.

When he finally went home that night, and lay in bed, he could think about nothing but Gina and what it had been like to hold her in his arms. Even now, he could still feel her; the softness and the warmth, the firmness of her shoulders, the heaving of her breasts.

✳

Frank angled his feet carefully between the struts of the gangplank, feeling the wood give and shudder like a live thing under the weight of the men stamping down it. He held his case in one hand and supported the old man with the other. He couldn't afford to stumble or ease his grip for even a second. If he did, the old man would almost certainly lose his balance and fall – so tightly, almost desperately, was he clutching Frank's arm. The boy, whose name was Josef, carried Carlo's bag as well as his own and stayed close behind them. He watched where the old man put his feet, ready to drop the bags and catch him if something did go wrong.

Across the harbour half a dozen fishing boats were unloading the morning's catch. A congregation of gulls was squabbling and squealing overhead, lurching abruptly down towards the boats and then sweeping effortlessly back up again at the last moment. Occasionally, a flurry of them followed a cascade of discarded fish down to the sea and churned the water white for a moment or two, screeching and snapping at each other.

The sun dazzled the men and there was a strong wind, which seemed to tug at their coats and jackets as if trying to steal them.

The gusting wind, the brightness of the light glancing off the sea like a mirror, the pungent smell of salt and oil; these were Frank's first impressions of the Isle of Man and they were what he remembered most vividly long after the war was over. To the surprise of some people, Frank always talked warmly and with affection about the island. He would encourage people to go there.

'The weans'll have a ball,' he would say. 'An' so will-a you. Beautiful place, so it is.'

He, of course, never went back.

'Can we-a stay together,' Frank said to the soldier The soldier took the three sets of papers and made some notes.

'That bunch there,' he said and then added, looking at Carlo. 'They're not going far.'

'Thanks,' Frank said and helped the old man to the group which the soldier had indicated. After a time, an officer and a soldier with his rifle slung over his shoulder approached their group. The officer stopped in front of them, hands behind his back, and nodded to them, smiling.

'Okay, men, let's move off. And do try to stay together please.'

It was a request, not an order. And Frank couldn't help but smile at the 'please'; so very British and somehow comforting, too. Maybe this wouldn't be so bad, after all. 'Just get through it,' he said to himself. That was all he had to do. Get through it.

They set off at an easy pace along the promenade, passing sunken flowerbeds which were still immaculately tended and planted up with a blousy municipal display of geraniums, begonias and dahlias even though there would be no holidaymakers that year or for many years to come. On their right, the great curve of beach was cordoned off with barbed wire. In most other respects, though, Douglas and the green hilly bay which cradled it looked utterly normal; the perfect picture postcard of a holiday town. Some of the locals stopped briefly to watch the internees. But, by now, most islanders were all too familiar with these weary columns of men. There was no longer anything in the least interesting or unusual about them.

Carlo had to stop and rest every ten or fifteen yards and they were soon lagging well behind the main group. The officer and soldier occasionally checked that they were still there. But they didn't shout or chase them up. The rest of the group headed towards a camp that was right on the promenade. A barbed wire fence ran all the way round a block of small hotels and boarding houses that looked directly onto the beach. They were Edwardian houses, terraced, with steps leading up to a tiled porch and their names etched in glass panels above the front door: Bay View, Bide-a-Wee, Clifton House and so on. Typically, they had a certain ostentation about them but this was nothing more than a superficial gloss; an unconvincing attempt to seem something more than they actually were. Their irredeemable shabbiness was particularly marked just then because everything of value – curtains, carpets and furniture – had been emptied out of them, leaving them naked and exposed.

By the time Frank and Josef arrived at the gate with the old man, the other internees had already been allocated to their rooms. The officer waited at the gate, hands on his hips, not at all impatient. Only now did Frank realise that he was very young, perhaps no more than twenty three or twenty four.

'We should have had you in a lorry,' said the officer apologetically. 'But transport's hard to come by.'

'We're here now,' said Frank. 'Where do we go? He needs to lie down.'

'There's a good room at the front, just one floor up in this one here,' the officer said, pointing to a house called Mansion House Hotel, though it bore little resemblance to any kind of a mansion. There were men lounging around the front of each house, sitting on the steps or the low parapet walls. They looked at Frank and Carlo and Josef with the kind of mild, passing curiosity with which you might watch the other members of the audience arriving in the theatre before a performance begins. Frank could tell, from the snatches of conversation which he caught, that this camp was mainly given over to Germans and Austrians. But there were some Italians, too, and there were other languages which he couldn't immediately place.

Three young men were sitting on the steps in front of their house. They were fit and tanned, hair cropped. They were sailors, the crew of a German merchant ship which had been impounded on the East Coast of Africa soon after the war had begun. The sailor on the lowest step stared up at Josef but made no attempt to move. Josef's eyes flared.

'Can we get by, please?' said Frank. 'The old man needs to lie down.'

The young man looked briefly at Frank and then back at Josef. Still he did not move. Nor did any of the others. Frank looked around for the British officer but he had disappeared. The only other soldier in sight was patrolling outside the fence. Suddenly, from the top of the steps, someone spoke in German. He was older than the other sailors, clearly someone in authority. The young men promptly rose and moved to the side of the steps.

'Thank you,' said Frank to the older man. The man nodded

but with no particular warmth. He did not offer to help and almost immediately disappeared back into the house. As they climbed the steps, Frank heard the young sailor saying something to Josef. It was just one word, spat out in a vicious whisper. Frank had barely heard it, focusing his attention on Carlo, and he understood very little German. But he could not mistake that word, nor what it meant.

'Juden.'

The room was narrow with a window at the far end looking out over the sea. It and the room next door had clearly once been part of the same room. The partition wall that now divided them sliced through the cornice and came down hard against the frame of the window. The main principles governing the conversion had been purely practical. Aesthetics had never figured in the equation for even a moment. The same spirit, or lack of it, was evident throughout the house. Everything was cheaply done and, where there was a problem, as with the seeping soil pipe in the toilet, it had been patched up rather than properly mended. The floorboards throughout the house were bare. They creaked and echoed whenever anyone so much as shifted their weight from one foot to another. Everything that could be removed had been removed; that was pretty much the general rule in all the houses.

They laid Carlo on the bed nearest the window. They tried him on his left and then turned him onto his right side. Frank often found that he was better on his right, with his knees drawn up towards his chest. Carlo resisted and protested during this, swatting weakly at them, pleading to be left alone. Eventually, his breathing became slightly easier and they covered him up and let him sleep.

An Italian from Bradford who was staying in the next room had walked in during this. He started telling them about the house. He spoke as if he already knew them and was merely continuing a conversation that had previously been interrupted. Mostly Germans and Austrians, he said. The sailors lived on the floor above and people gave them a wide berth. Frank and Josef – particularly Josef, he said – should do likewise. They could collect their food from the stores and cook it downstairs. They should get their own pots and plates and keep them in the room. Anything left in the kitchen would vanish. It was best, too, he said, to avoid being in the kitchen at the same time as the sailors. Their captain, presumably the older man who'd spoken downstairs, kept them in line but he wasn't always around and, besides, you couldn't rely on him.

Frank listened to the man, whose name was Freddo, and whom he knew meant well. But his attention was all on Carlo. The old man was still noisy, the fluid in his lungs crackling and popping quietly with each breath. Frank used to say that no matter how deeply Carlo breathed, you never felt as if he was drawing in enough oxygen. And as you listened to him, you could feel your own lungs tighten as if the same thing was happening to you, too. Eventually Freddo stopped talking and, after a few moments of silence, returned to his own room. Josef disappeared for ten minutes or so and, when he came back, he was carrying an upright wooden chair which he placed beside Carlo's bed. Frank smiled and nodded his thanks. He would spend many hours in that chair, his eyes moving from Carlo to the glittering, grey sea until another bout of coughing or a change in the rhythm of his breathing brought him back to Carlo again.

★

Robert Glen came to the café first thing in the morning. Miller was wiping down the shelf below where the mirror had been. He'd cleared away the jars and bottles that were displayed here and now he was carefully gathering up the last fragments of mirror. Apart from the missing mirror, the café was pretty much back to normal. Miller had put the 'Closed' sign on the door but it wasn't locked and Robert naturally paid no attention to the sign.

'You okay?' he said, as he entered.

'Aye, fine,' said Miller, sweeping a tiny heap of glass shards into his cupped left hand and then emptying this into the bucket at his feet. He dusted his fingers lightly over the palm of his left hand to remove the pieces of glass that remained there, slightly embedded in the skin.

'What about Gina?'

'Aye, she's coped with it okay. She's been good. Have a word with her yoursel',' and he turned towards the kitchen door and called out, 'Gina!'

She emerged hesitantly from the kitchen, wary and unsure until she saw Robert.

'How are you, pet?' he said, coming over to the counter and taking off his cap.

'I'm all right. It was nothing.'

Robert shook his head, gently disagreeing with her.

'The boys told me what happened, said the place was in some state last night.'

Gina shrugged and looked over at Miller.

'It wasnae that bad, was it, Ian?'

Miller shook his head.

'No, we've got most of it cleaned up,' he said. 'Mirror was the worst casualty.'

The policeman looked at Miller as if he was only just noticing him for the first time.

'You know, he offered to pay for this. Blair did,' said Robert.

'I don't want that,' said Gina firmly.

'He offered. It wasnae us.'

She shook her head.

'What happened to him?' she asked.

'We kept him in for a couple of hours until he sobered up. Then his brother came and took him home. He was in a terrible way. But really sorry for a' this.'

'This is nothin' compared to what he's lost.'

'Aye well, you have any problem replacin' that . . . You know, wi' the shortages an that. You let me know.' Robert said to Gina.

'It's okay,' Miller said. 'I've been on the phone this morning. I've got another one ordered. Payin' a bit over the odds. But we just want the place lookin' like it did as soon as we can.'

'Good,' said Robert after a moment. 'Best thing.'

'Come and have a cup of tea with me,' said Gina. 'I've got some scones due out of the oven any minute now.'

'Wish I could, pet. I'm just so busy an' I've got that much paperwork. These older blokes they're bringin' back to replace them that have gone tae the army are okay. But they cannae handle the paperwork. I tell you, I'm drownin' there. But I swear that I'll look in soon. Honest tae God.'

'Anytime,' said Gina.

'That's a promise,' said Robert, heading back to the door.

'Robert?' she said.

He stopped, knowing what she was going to ask.

'You've no' had any word of Frank?'

'Sorry, pet, nothin' at all.'

'I know you would have said. I'm sorry for asking.'

'It's okay. I just wish I could tell you something. No letters yet?'

'No.'

'You'll hear soon, I'm sure you will. An' I'm sure he's okay.'

'Aye,' said Gina.

'Hey, you sound right Scottish when you say that,' he said, grinning at her.

'I suppose that's something, eh?'

'Aye, so it is. We'll get you learned yet, eh?'

'Aye,' she repeated, smiling shyly.

'You just take care of yourself,' he said, suddenly serious. 'And I will be back soon. I promise.'

She watched him, through the windows, hurrying down the street until he disappeared out of sight.

'He's a good man,' she said, as she turned back into the kitchen.

'Aye, so he is,' said Miller.

They opened later than usual that Saturday and they cut the lunchtime menu back to just two main dishes. Most people knew what had happened the night before and those who didn't soon heard. It was curious but it made quite a difference to the café, the mirror being gone; the place was suddenly smaller, darker, almost drab. There was no doubt that business dropped away over the couple of weeks before they were able to replace the mirror. That could have been because the trouble with Blair reminded people about The Bay of Naples and the Italian flags and pictures that Frank had around the walls. But both Gina and

Miller felt it had something to do with the mirror. In truth, even after the mirror was replaced (though, of course, they couldn't get one exactly the same), business never entirely picked up again for a long time. Then again, there could have been lots of reasons for that.

Once she had started into the hard work of the day, keeping up with orders, sending out the meals at the right time, Gina felt better and was able, most of the time, to forget the events of last night. There was nothing else she could do, no one else she could turn to. In the past, after the war had started and while the men were still at home, the Italian families would visit each other as soon as they heard there'd been trouble. But the men were all gone now and the women were cautious about going out. The Ravezzis in Greenock were still keeping their café going under a different name but Gina hadn't seen them for months and hadn't spoken to them on the telephone for almost as long. Everyone had their own problems, Gina knew that all too well. She still hoped that one of the Italian women in the town, or even one of the Ravezzis, who would surely have heard, would call in that afternoon, maybe in the quiet spell before they started serving tea. But no one did. And Gina knew that she had been foolish to hope for it. She was on her own now and she had to manage on her own.

Miller had been watching her closely. There were several moments during the day when he felt certain of a shift in her attitude towards him. She smiled at him more often and more readily. And she had deferred to him over the business of the mirror, left that completely up to him. She had also, he was sure, been more comfortable and relaxed when she was close to him. No, there was no doubt in Miller's mind that last night had altered things between them. And he ached with pleasure when he recalled, almost as if she were still there, the sensation of holding her in his arms.

They went through the usual end-of-the-day routine of cleaning up silently and separately. When he had finished in the café, he came through to the kitchen where she was putting away the last few gleaming pans.

'I'm glad we got through today without any bother,' she said, smiling at him. 'Aren't you?'

'Aye, I am,' he said, the words thick in his throat.

'Time to call it a day, don't you think?'

He nodded as she dried her hands with her apron.

'How are you feeling?' he asked.

'You mean – about last night?'

'Aye,' he said, moving closer to her.

'I'm fine, Ian,' she said, looking at him, slightly perplexed. 'Really, I am.'

He nodded and took her hand in his. She didn't withdraw her hand or try to move away from him. Which confirmed him, instantly, in his belief that she had felt exactly what he had felt when they embraced the previous night.

'You don't need to worry about me, Ian,' she said after a moment. He smiled and pressed her hand more tightly, clasping it now between both his hands. She had allowed him, initially, to take her hand because the suddenness of the gesture had surprised her; but also, partly, because it had seemed like a characteristically awkward expression of concern and sympathy. But the moment had moved beyond that, taking them suddenly into different territory entirely. There was something shocking and deeply personal in the way he pressed the tips of his fingers into her skin, was now trying to work his fingers intimately between hers. There was, too, the look in his eyes. That had nothing to do with either concern or sympathy. And now with his free arm he was trying to embrace her, draw her even closer to him.

'What are you doing?' she said, stepping back. He held onto her hand for a moment more, easily stronger than her, then released it. He was still smiling, not yet having grasped what was happening.

She was shaking her head and backing away from him, her elbows tight against her body and her palms open as if to push him away. And now, as if time had slowed right down, he gradually registered the look in her eyes: a kind of horror, something not far short of revulsion. There was no mistaking this. Absolutely none. The smile drained away from his face. And he felt sick to his stomach, literally about to vomit.

'I'm sorry,' he said, staring at the cold linoleum floor, frantically trying to backtrack, believing that he could still wind the clock back and erase the shadow of the last few moments. 'I was just sayin'' – I hope you're okay. That's a'.'

But the lie sounded hopelessly feeble and false even to his ears. The clock wouldn't, couldn't, be turned back. He couldn't look at her now. He couldn't risk meeting her eyes. He started shuffling backwards out of the kitchen but almost tripped over his feet and had to grab at the edge of the draining board to stop himself falling.

'I'll lock up and head off,' he said as he reached the doorway, like a drowning man coming up for air again. She didn't respond, was simply too terrified to open her mouth and speak. He knew that, could sense it all too clearly without even laying eyes on her. As soon as he left the kitchen, she went upstairs. Out in the café, his eyes filling with tears, he heard her close and lock the door to the upstairs flat. He switched off the remaining lights and left by the front door, locking it after him, as he normally did. Then he hurried home, keeping close to the walls of the tenements, taking the back road rather than the more direct way straight up Causeyside Street, his skin burning with shame and hurt and humiliation.

✳

Fortunately, the next day was Sunday and the café was closed. Which gave them both some time to think about what had happened. Gina knew that, as a woman on her own, she should have been more vigilant, more on her guard. It had been up to her, Gina felt, to watch out for any undue attention. And she would do that from now on. She wouldn't mention this on Monday. She changed her mind about this many times in the course of the day but decided, in the end, that this would be the best way to handle it. One thing was quite certain, though, she wouldn't let this happen again. It had been that business on Friday night, when she broke down and fell into his arms. She knew now, no matter what difficulties or problems they encountered, she had to deal with them on her own. She couldn't show anyone else, especially not Miller, what she felt. She had to wait for Frank. When he came home, everything would be different. She could tell him anything and everything. And she could cry in his arms as much as she wanted, though she hoped she wouldn't do much of that. She wouldn't tell him about this either, she decided. She would just let it go. On Monday, when Miller came, it would be as if it had never happened. That was how they would deal with it.

It didn't occur to her until Monday morning that Miller might *not* come back. Which would give her a whole other set of problems. She was lying in bed, suddenly dismayed by this previously unconsidered possibility, when she heard noises from downstairs. It was a quarter past six, well before they usually started work. But someone was bringing in the milk crates from the back door where the milkman had left them just after five; she had been awake then, as she had been throughout much of the night. She went through to the back bedroom and looked out of the window. After a moment, Miller came into sight, crossing the small yard and lifting another crate to carry it into the café. She was relieved and pleased. She felt sure, watching him disappear back into the café, that things would be okay. Once they'd picked their way through the initial embarrassment of the morning, everything would be fine. They would revert to the way things had been before, or at least the way they'd been ever since Frank left. She washed and dressed quickly and went downstairs.

'Morning,' she said as she came into the kitchen.

'Morning,' he said quietly, keeping his eyes down.

'How are you?' she asked as she put on her apron.

'Fine,' he said, carrying some lemonade bottles out to the counter, still not looking at her. This was all right, though. They could go on from here without any trouble, she thought. It was just a case of getting on with it.

Miller kept at it all that day. In fact, for the next week or so, he threw himself into his work even more than ever before. It was almost as if, it seemed to her, he was trying to atone for that night. And, at first, this was exactly what was in Miller's mind. He would show her how well he could work. He would expunge the memory of that mistake. And, in that way, he would make it up to Frank and Gina. Everything would be just as it had been before.

It wasn't until two or maybe three weeks later that he began to feel differently about this incident, though that awkward fumbled attempt at intimacy was never far from his thoughts. It hadn't been his fault, he told himself. A mistake, that's all it had been. Perhaps it hadn't even been a mistake. Women are like that; they can chop and change, lead you on and stop you in your tracks, go this way and that so you never know where you stand with them. Despite the pain it had caused him, it obviously hadn't bothered her. She'd never mentioned it, never once even alluded to it. So why, he reasoned, should he continue to punish himself, lacerate himself, over something that seemed not to have troubled her? Why try to atone when there was nothing to atone for? It wasn't as if he owed Gina or Frank anything now. Frank had been good to him in the past but he had repaid that debt many times over by now. He had helped them out when she had the miscarriage and he had helped her keep the place open ever since Frank was taken. She couldn't have managed it on her own. She still couldn't manage it without him. No, he didn't owe anyone anything now. He had no reason to be sorry for a few absurd moments that hadn't meant anything to anyone. No reason at all.

★

Later that first day, when Carlo had settled into a deep sleep, Frank went off to claim their food and bedding from the stores. This, like everything else, took time, and involved waiting in queues, having their names checked off on various lists. When he came back to the house, Frank made a stew of beef and potatoes. Some of the sailors came into the kitchen while he was there. They were neither friendly nor unfriendly. They sat at the table and talked, mostly in German. They didn't say anything to Frank. It was almost as if he wasn't there but then Frank had noticed that internment often bred this strange indifference towards each other among the men around him. You had no privacy but there was also no obligation on you to be particularly sociable. If a man sat next to you, you did not need to talk to him. And if the voluble Freddo had wandered into their room, as he had that morning, he did not feel obliged to introduce himself or explain why he'd finally decided to leave again. It must be a bit like this in prison, Frank thought. Then he laughed at himself, shaking his head; it must be *exactly* like this, Frank thought, because that's exactly what this is.

The kitchen was small and pokey and the cooker wasn't very different to what you might have in an ordinary house. How anyone had ever turned out three meals a day for twenty five or thirty guests in a kitchen like this was beyond Frank. But then, in that sense, the kitchen and the cooker were on a par with the rest of the house. And Frank saw now, with a touch more sympathy than he'd felt at first, just how much of a struggle it must have been to make a living out of this place – especially when you were cheek by jowl with dozens of other boarding houses and small hotels, any of which could undercut you by a few shillings a week or steal your bookings for next summer by offering a radio in the lounge or cream cakes with the eleven o'clock tea.

Frank couldn't get Carlo to eat the stew. The boy tried too but was no more successful. If anything, the effort of waking him and sitting him up in bed seemed to make him worse. His breathing became fast and shallow. The phlegmy, painful-sounding coughing started again. Freddo and some of the other internees in the house materialised at the back of the room or in the doorway, usually saying very little, sometimes nothing at all. They watched for a time and then just as silently left again. There was so little for any of them to do that even the sight of infirmity counted as a kind of entertainment or, at least, a distraction. Here, too, there was that same indifference, that sense that it was unnecessary to explain their coming or going because, after all, what could any of them actually *do*?

Around eleven o'clock, Carlo's breathing became so bad that Frank began to wonder if he would survive the night. Frank and the boy tried moving him, first onto one side and then onto the other. They propped him up in bed with extra pillows and then laid him flat without any pillows at all. But none of this helped him or eased him in any way. Eventually, despite the curfew, which had begun at nine thirty, Frank went into the street and shouted to the soldiers that they needed a doctor in the house and they needed him now.

'Get back in your house,' a soldier shouted from the guard room on the ground floor of the house nearest the gate. Frank didn't care if they locked him up or shot him, he said. He wasn't moving until they brought a doctor. Eventually, the sergeant on duty went with Frank to look at Carlo.

'Aye, okay, okay,' he said, standing at the foot of Carlo's bed but not going any closer. The sergeant was a cocky, barrel-chested bantam of a man called Burke. He had a Newcastle accent and blue eyes that glinted deep in their sockets with a kind of wary slyness. He stopped for a moment before leaving and stared at Frank as if Frank had somehow won this contest and he had lost. What's more, he seemed to be indicating, he wouldn't forget it, either.

The doctor arrived twenty minutes later. He had retired several years ago but had, as he said, 're-enlisted' because the war had created a shortage of doctors on the island. He gave Carlo oxygen which finally eased his breathing. He left the canister of oxygen and gave them medicine but said this would only help with the symptoms, not cure the underlying problem. Carlo had late stage emphysema, he told them, and there was precious little anyone could do about that. If Carlo became worse, the doctor would admit him to hospital. But even there, they couldn't do much. The best thing he could do was to rest and eat and generally build up his strength.

Gradually in the course of that day, their second in the house, Carlo finally became more settled and was breathing almost normally. In the evening, he even took some weak soup. It was while he was taking this that Frank heard a sudden commotion downstairs. Almost as soon as the shouting and thumping began, he knew what it was.

Sure enough, as he came round the turn of the stairs, he saw Josef lashing out at a group of the sailors. They were standing round him in a circle, punching and kicking at him. As he turned to deal with one of them, another would hit him from behind. The young sailor who'd called him a Jew spat at him, the spit landing on the back of Josef's neck and trickling down. Josef suddenly launched himself at the young sailor, causing both of them to go crashing against the front door and twisting onto the floor. Josef had somehow clamped himself onto the sailor, having landed on top of him, and was pummelling him with his fists. The other sailors rushed in, kicking and punching Josef, who seemed to feel nothing. Frank shouldered them aside and grabbed the collar of Josef's jacket, twisting it in his hand to give himself a better grip and ensure he had Josef's full attention.

'That's enough,' shouted Frank.

'But they –,' began Josef.

'I don't care. I don't want to hear another word. Enough!'

Now most of the other inhabitants of the house were looking over the banisters or standing at the door of the kitchen. Frank backed up the stairs, dragging Josef with him. The sailors were wiping their faces, breathing heavily. They'd been taken by surprise at Frank's decisive and confident intervention. The young sailor was bleeding from his nose and mouth, nostrils flaring. The sailors were beginning to move towards the stairs, coming after Frank and Josef when the captain pushed his way through the kitchen doorway and said something in German. The sailors stopped but they did not back down. He repeated himself, louder this time. They nodded and filed angrily outside, glaring back at Frank and particularly at Josef.

'Speak to them,' Frank said to the captain.

'I already have.'

'Well, do it again. We're all stuck here for the time being. We need to behave like human beings, not animals.'

'I agree.'

'Good,' said Frank. He didn't feel entirely convinced by the German captain but there was nothing more he could think to say at that moment. He turned to Josef and started pushing him up the stairs, as if he was a child.

'Move!' he shouted. 'Now!'

The next morning, Frank went into each of the twenty or

so houses in the camp. He asked if there were any spare rooms. But most of the rooms were taken by that time. The few that were left were up three or four flights of stairs or so small that they would be no good for three of them. He went to the guard house and asked Burke if they could be moved to another camp. When Burke asked why, he told them about the sailors and the trouble they'd caused with the boy because he was Jewish. Burke laughed quietly and dismissively. He told Frank that no one could be moved; maybe later they might manage it but not then. Frank persisted, growing more and more agitated. 'You need to move us,' he heard himself finally shouting at Burke, leaning across the desk towards him. Burke merely shook his head, 'No, I don't.' And Frank could see, in his eyes, how much pleasure he took from this moment and how much he enjoyed this petty exercising of his absolute power.

They would have to make the best of things. And so they cautiously did. There was no more trouble between Josef and the sailors – not at that time, anyway. The old man continued to improve and they soon discovered that life here was more comfortable than it had been in any of the other camps. They had good food; the meat and vegetables were excellent and, apparently, abundant. They were able to cook for themselves when and how they wanted. And their room was slowly becoming more like a home of sorts as Josef kept returning from his travels with items such as a standard lamp, a bookcase, books, cushions, a little armchair. And then, of course, the best thing of all happened.

When the soldier called his name at the morning post reveille, Frank was shocked and initially wary, afraid that it might simply be a mistake or that the letter could be for some other

Jaconelli. He took the letter from the soldier and recognised her handwriting at once. He hurried over to a quiet part of the street overlooking the beach and took a moment before he opened it. The envelope had been stamped over countless times as it had been redirected up and down the country. It had been opened and re-sealed with tape which read 'Opened by Censor'. He saw, from the postmark, that it had been posted on the 15th of July. When he read the letter, it was clear that this wasn't her first one but that didn't matter in the least. It consisted of three closely packed pages in Gina's tiny but elegant handwriting. Exactly as taught by the nuns. To his amazement and delight, the letter was telling him that the café had reopened. That Gina was running the place with Miller's help. And that business was picking up every day. He read the letter over several times and he could tell, from what she wrote, that she was all right. She wasn't worried or anxious. She was keeping herself busy and making a living. He told himself that the letter was over two months old. But, even so, it was better – far better – than he had ever hoped. Frank tucked the letter into his shirt pocket and walked back to the house to tell Carlo his news.

✳

Gina didn't keep any running check on how much was, or should be, in the till. You couldn't do that in the café. With so many small transactions, you could never hope to match stock going out with cash coming in. Or, rather, it would have taken so much time that you couldn't do anything else. Even so, Gina had learned over the last few months to gauge the till float fairly precisely with just the quickest of glances. She could tell, with a degree of accuracy that often surprised her, whether the till contained £53 or £55. And she had a good sense now of what ought to be in there at the end of each day, depending on which day of the week it was. Friday was usually their best day, Saturday next, Monday their worst. That particular night, being a Tuesday, they should have taken around £47 or £48. And half an hour before they closed, Gina had opened the till to sell someone five Capstan. She hadn't looked at the money closely and it was impossible, of course, to remember exactly what she'd seen. But her feeling had been that they'd done reasonably well for a Tuesday. She thought they might even have edged up to around the £50 mark. However, when she went upstairs and cashed up on the kitchen table in the flat, she found that she had just £44 17s 8d in front of her. She checked and re-checked the money but it came to the same total each time.

At first, she was convinced that Miller had taken the money. She felt sick and frightened and barely slept that night, dreaded the thought of seeing him again the next day. But in the morning, when she thought about it more calmly, she realised that she could have been mistaken, more than likely *was* mistaken. Maybe it had been less busy than usual yesterday. Maybe she hadn't looked closely enough at the money in the till when she opened it. She had absolutely no evidence to suggest that any money was missing, never mind that Miller had taken it. And she began to feel that she had been foolish, even a little hysterical.

Gina knew that you couldn't read someone's heart by watching what they do. What happens on the surface, what people allow you to see, is no very reliable guide to what's going on inside, behind the shutters that we throw up between ourselves and other people. But she still felt that, if Miller had taken money, he would betray himself in some small way. He wouldn't be able to help it. There would be something different in his manner or attitude towards her. She would know.

Although she watched him closely over the next few days, she couldn't see any change in him. His manner towards her neither softened nor hardened. He remained slightly cool and distant, as he had been ever since the business of the attempted embrace, almost as if he was the one who'd been hurt. He took a little longer perhaps to do what she asked him to do but he always did it. And he was never actually rude or disrespectful towards her. During this time, she was also keeping a closer eye on the till float, counting it more often during the day. But there were no more discrepancies. And, as the days passed, Gina became convinced that she'd been wrong. She'd allowed her imagination to get the better of her. Also, and equally importantly, she wanted to be fair to Miller. Apart from that single unfortunate misunderstanding, Miller had been a godsend to both her and Frank. He had kept the café going single-handedly when she had the miscarriage. And, without his help, she could never have reopened the café after Frank had been interned. It was true that now she could probably manage without him; she knew the basics and could almost certainly find someone else to take his place. But that wasn't the point. She wanted to be scrupulously fair, just as Frank would have been. And she wanted to keep things as they were, if she possibly could, until Frank came home. Any day now, if they were lucky, Frank could come walking back through the front door of the café. And he would pick her up in his arms, lift her off the floor, hold her tight against his chest for minutes that would seem like an eternity. And she would bury her face in his shoulder and cry. He would laugh at her and then they would kiss and she'd taste the salt of her own tears in the kiss. Until that day, though, Gina wouldn't upset things in the café. She would keep going. Think of Frank and keep going.

✶

It hadn't been the first time he had taken money from the till. But it was the first time he'd taken so much. Before that, it had been just a few shillings, nothing she'd ever miss. He'd started taking the money in the last couple of weeks of September. By that time, he knew he was safe and that she wasn't going to tell Robert Glen or anyone else. Even if she did say something now, it would carry less weight. People would wonder why, if it had really bothered her, she hadn't said anything about it at the time. His position was, if anything, stronger than it had been before. As they moved into October, he felt more sure of himself, more in control of things, as if the balance of power between them had shifted subtly but significantly. The money was just part of that. As he saw it now, they owed him the money anyway. It was his by rights. He was worth much more than she was paying him. It had been him that kept the café going. Without him there would be no café. The money, a few pounds here and there, was the least he was due.

He knew that he'd taken too much that Tuesday night. He could tell the following morning from a certain tenseness in her. And she was watching him more closely than usual, he was quite sure of that. He'd taken the money too late in the day: four pounds and some silver, all at once, just before they closed up for the night. He wouldn't make that mistake again. He took very little for the next few days. And then he was careful to take it at different times during the day, often in silver, never more than ten shillings at a time. He knew, as the days went on, that she wasn't watching him so much any more. She'd obviously decided she'd made a mistake. And he wasn't going to take that chance again. He hadn't even needed the money for anything. He didn't know why he'd taken so much. It was almost, he sometimes thought, as if he wanted her to find out. But that made no sense. No, he would go on taking the money. He would take what he felt she owed him. But he would do it so carefully and gradually that she wouldn't have any idea what was happening.

As they moved towards the end of October, this was pretty much how things were working out. He continued to take money. Gina noticed nothing and had virtually forgotten that she ever suspected him. She wished that they could somehow clear the air between them. But he still turned up every day. And he worked reasonably hard. In the end, that was as much as she could expect. As the days and weeks ground on, she found herself hoping more and more for Frank's return. Surely they couldn't keep him much longer? When Frank came back, he would sort this out. She wouldn't need to worry about the café or Miller. Frank would take care of it all. This was more or less what she was thinking on the afternoon of the last Friday in October around two o'clock. The lunchtime rush was over and there would be a lull before people started coming in for tea and cakes. There were a few people still lingering in the café, finishing late meals. Miller had been talking to them the last time she looked out. Out on the main road, a convoy of army trucks and jeeps was going by. There were people standing outside the windows of the café watching them. They had started going by about twenty minutes ago and she could still hear the lorries grinding by in low gear as they went down the slight slope of the hill into Causeyside Street.

She finished washing the plates and, drying her hands on her apron, moved across the kitchen to the door that opened into the café. It was presumably the noise of the lorries that prevented Miller from hearing her. As she reached the half-open door and was about to pull it towards her, she caught sight of him at the till. The drawer was open. He lifted a ten-shilling note by the corner and folded it into his hand. Then he slipped his hand into his trouser pocket and drew it out again, a moment later, empty.

5

Every morning, the sailors exercised vigorously for an hour or so in the street outside the house. These exercises were strictly limited to German or Polish seamen, of whom there was a fairly large contingent in the camp. Some mornings, there were thirty-five or forty men clattering and grunting their way through a long, testing programme of sit-ups, press-ups, stretches and gymnastics. They did this in all weathers, stripped to their vests and trousers. Often, as they moved into autumn, they were soaked through by the rain in the course of their session. But the weather was no excuse to ease up or stop and they kept up the same daunting pace regardless. The captain called out instructions in German and performed each exercise as wholeheartedly as any of his charges. There was a clear competitive edge to these sessions. Every so often, some little contest would break out among a group of the men. They would grin, laugh or shout in painful exhilaration as they pushed and tested each other. Who could do the fastest sit-ups? Or the most press-ups? Who could do the best back vaults and the most controlled landing? Despite the laughter and the smiles, there was no doubting their seriousness nor the strength of their desire to win. They were young, fit men with energy to burn. And this was their way of working at least some of it off.

They also had regular boxing matches. Two men at a time, with strips of carpet wrapped round their knuckles instead of gloves, would fight each other in a ring formed by the sailors. The audience would be augmented by other internees drawn by the simple fact that something was happening to break the monotony of their day. Men hung out of windows to give themselves a better view. The soldiers, too, usually came out onto the top of the steps outside their office and watched in silence. They were bloody but short contests. The captain kept a close eye on each bout and never allowed them to go beyond the point where one man had clearly demonstrated his superiority over another. No one ever disputed his authority. When he asked for the boxers to break or stop, they invariably did so.

The young sailor who'd been provoking Josef often took part in these boxing matches. He was Polish and his name was Marek. He would sometimes take on two or three men in a row and generally won. He was on the slim side, his torso tightly muscled. He had high, angular cheekbones which almost poked through his skin. He was, Frank thought, only nineteen or twenty and he displayed that particular coldness which only such young men possess. Truly dead eyes, especially when he was fighting. There had continued to be tension between Marek and Josef but it had not so far caused any more problems. Frank knew that the hostile looks between the two young men and the 'accidental', bundling shoves as they passed each other on the stairs would inevitably lead to trouble. There was no chance that a situation like this could turn out any other way. It was simply a matter now of where and when and how.

One morning, late in September, Frank had been out with Josef waiting by the guardhouse to see if a letter had come. Josef wasn't expecting any letters from anyone but he was happy to keep Frank company. Naturally, the soldier who read out the names of those who had letters mangled most of them. So those who didn't have letters sometimes thought that they did and those who did have letters often thought that they didn't, not realising that their names had been called. The internees had learned that here, too, they must find a way of working round their situation. Anyone who hoped for a letter and had a modicum of sense waited till this procedure was over and then took their turn looking through the letters which the soldier was still holding. Then, you would often hear something like the following exchange. An internee would stab at a letter and say his name which was, to him, written clearly on the front of the envelope in question; at this, the soldier would shrug and say, 'Oh, *that's* how you pronounce it?'

When Frank had looked through the letters, he finally accepted that there really was nothing for him that morning. But there was still a boxing match in progress outside the house so they waited where they were till it was over. It was a sunny day with the promise of winter in the sharp, blustery wind. Frank and Josef watched, with a kind of mild envy, two boys digging for bait on the beach. They came down quite often, ignoring the internees and the camp, and generally kept to much the same spot. When they had enough worms, they walked out to the headland beyond the harbour where they tried to catch the eels that swirled around the rocks and brushed through the seaweed, their powerful snaking bodies glinting blackly in the sea. Frank had never actually seen the boys catch one but then they were quite far away. And he could only pick them out by their shapes and the colour of their jumpers or jackets. Whether they did catch anything or not, they kept it up, appearing every few days, a welcome reminder of the everyday world that still existed on the other side of the barbed wire.

When the boxing match was over, and the crowd outside the house was beginning to drift away, he and Josef headed back towards the house. Marek was sitting on the wall, unwrapping a strip of carpet from his left hand. Frank and Josef started up the steps that led to the front door. Suddenly, something slapped against Josef's shoulder. Frank turned and saw the strip of bloody carpet, which Marek had thrown at Josef, lying a few steps below them. Marek said something in Polish. Frank seized Josef's arm and pushed him up the stairs.

'He asks if you would fight him,' the captain said.

'No, no fighting,' Frank said, drawing Josef towards the door. Josef hung reluctantly back, going with Frank but looking down at the sailors. Marek said something else and grinned.

'What did he say?' asked Josef.

'He says you are frightened of him – a coward,' said the captain.

'No, we're no' fighting,' said Frank, on the top step now. 'Come on, you.'

But Josef shook his head and yanked his arm out of Frank's grip. No one spoke for a good long moment or so.

'It will be fair,' said the captain. 'I give you my word.'

Frank could see that the German meant this. But he was also pleased, and perhaps a little surprised, that Josef had allowed himself to be so easily suckered into the challenge. Frank reached out towards the boy, trying to catch his shoulder, but

Josef was already moving down the stairs to where a sailor was holding out several strips of carpet to him.

Frank watched, appalled, as they went through their preparations, squared up to each other and then began remorselessly to lay into each other with their fists. The strips of carpet fell from their hands within the first minute or so and still they kept going. They were bleeding, crying out – sometimes both at the same time – as each punch landed. All of the soldiers, not just one or two, came out of the office and stood watching. Everyone who had walked off earlier came back, drawing even more people with them. After a few minutes – none of these bouts lasted for very much longer – it became clear that a strange thing was happening. Marek was taller than Josef and stronger. But Josef was getting the upper hand. No one watching could doubt that. The reason was simple: he was indifferent to the hurt that the young sailor was inflicting on him. Frank – who never liked violence and avoided witnessing it, when he could – had sometimes seen the same thing in street fights in Paisley on a Friday or Saturday night. Given that all else was equal, the winner was the one who cared least about being hurt. That was what was happening here: Marek cared very little but Josef cared even less.

Josef's dark eyes were focused only on the sailor. And as often as he was pushed away and knocked to the ground, he came back. He was constantly landing his own punches, catching Marek on the body, on the face, wherever he could. It seemed as if they had been fighting for hours but in fact it was only four or five minutes. The young sailor was leaning back against the crowd, which had begun to grow quieter again. But they mercilessly pushed him back towards Josef. And Josef continued to come at him, unrelenting even now that he had the advantage. Marek was bleeding from the mouth and from a bad cut above his right eye. He could barely see, could barely stand. Suddenly, the captain pushed through the crowd and placed himself between Josef and the young sailor. The men in the ring protested. Marek tried feebly to brush past the captain, willing to continue. But the captain whispered a few angry words to him. Marek turned away and sat on the wall, no one helping him.

For the next few days, things were tense in the house. They did not see much of Marek but, when they did, it was clear that this was far from finished. On the third night after the fight, Josef went down to the kitchen to fill a large enamel jug with water. They kept this in their room and drank from it during the day. The kitchen was empty, the sailors sitting out on the steps as usual. But when Josef stepped into the hall, Marek suddenly came at him. He felt a burning sensation on his arm and the jug fell from his hand. Marek was holding a knife. It was an ordinary kitchen knife sharpened to a point and with tape wrapped round the handle. Josef realised now that he'd been cut on the arm and was bleeding. He faced up to Marek, keeping his eye on the knife. Then, with no warning, someone lunged at Marek from the doorway, throwing him forward onto the floor. And the captain was standing over him, ripping the knife from his fingers, bending them back to release it.

'I am sorry,' said the captain. Josef nodded and picked up the jug. He went back upstairs without bothering to refill it. That could wait. Frank was already waiting at the turn of the stairs for him. Frank put his arm round the boy's shoulder and they walked back to their room. As they did so, Frank could feel the boy's body trembling with shock.

The next day Marek was gone. He had been moved by the captain to another house, further along the street. They still saw him every day and his hatred of Josef was evident. But he kept his distance from them and from their house, for which Frank was grateful.

As they moved into November, life became a little easier for them. The old man improved, though never so much that Frank could stop worrying. He still had regular, agonising spasms of coughing and times when he couldn't seem to draw a breath. When this happened, either Frank or the boy would give him the oxygen and sit with him until the attack passed. But otherwise things were relatively bearable. They were together and their room in the boarding house was warm and comfortable. Marek was gone and the other sailors generally avoided Josef. No, there was much for which to be grateful. And, of course, Frank was feeling slightly better about Gina.

By early November, he had received eight letters from her. These had arrived haphazardly, out of sequence, so it was sometimes difficult for him to grasp what she was saying in one letter when she was clearly referring to something she'd written in another letter which hadn't arrived yet. This however was a minor irritation compared to the deep pleasure which these small, creased, densely-covered sheets of paper brought him. He kept them tucked away in a corner in his case and took them out regularly to read over again or just to hold. The letters created, briefly, the feeling of being with Gina. But, of course, it was just an illusion. He could read the letters as often as he wanted but it was nothing like hearing her voice, nothing like holding her hand or touching her skin, nothing like fitting his body against hers as they lay in bed. Carlo, whose wife had died eight years before, understood much of what Frank was feeling. He still missed his own wife, couldn't quite believe she really had gone. Most mornings, when he woke, his first impulse was to reach over towards her in the bed and it was only then he would remember. There was some part of his mind, it seemed, that would never accept the fact of her death. So he knew how much Frank must miss Gina and how much he worried about her. Every so often, when Frank was feeling low, Carlo would say, 'Be patient, Frank. Wait it out. You'll see her again.'

'Aye, I'm-a sure you're right. Patience . . . patience . . .'

By that time, Frank was reconciled to the fact that he would probably stay on the Isle of Man for quite some time. And he accepted that his only course of action was to wait and let things work themselves through in their own good time. He was fairly philosophical about things and still believed that this would work out okay in the end.

All of that changed for Frank when the next letter arrived.

The previous letters had been written during the summer. This one had somehow slipped ahead of others that were presumably lost or stuck in the post. It had been written at the end of October, just a week ago. Frank knew there was something different about this letter the moment he saw the handwriting on the envelope. It was shaky and uneven; maybe just hastily written to catch the post, he thought at first.

There was only one sheet in the envelope and she had finished the letter halfway down the second side. Usually she crammed each page full, sometimes fitting little postscripts, in tiny writing, in any gaps that she'd left after signing her name and adding a couple of rows of x's. Her handwriting was difficult to read, which had never been the case before. This wasn't the copper-plate which the nuns had taught her, with the aid of sharp raps across the knuckles with a wooden ruler. This was nothing like the other letters where you could hear Gina saying exactly what she had written on her page, as if the ink and the words were a cage to capture her voice. From what he could make out, the café was still open and she was working hard every day, Sundays excepted. She didn't mention Miller, though, and that troubled Frank because she had always done so in the other letters, emphasising how much of a help he had been and saying how she could never have managed without him. Had he left? Was she trying to run the place on her own? Of course, she wouldn't tell him that; she wouldn't want to worry him. He couldn't be sure what it was but something was wrong. Something had changed.

He went back to the house, opened the suitcase and took out the bundle of letters. The latest one had been written on the 3rd of September. He flattened it out with his hand and laid it beside this new letter. The same blue paper. The same black ink. And there was, naturally, a similarity in the handwriting. But you could almost believe they had been written by different people. What had happened to her? Was it Miller? Was she on her own now? Or was it something else entirely?

Frank wrote to her that afternoon. His letter was longer than usual, full of questions, urging her to be open with him, to ask for help if she needed it. He reminded her of the people whom she could trust: Robert Glen, the priest, the Ravezzis in Gourock. He hoped he was wrong, he wrote to her. Maybe she'd just been tired after a long day in the café. The last thing he wanted to do was upset her by jumping to conclusions. But he was worried. And he wasn't about to deny it or pretend otherwise. He decided that he would write to the Ravezzis, too.

They may not have seen Gina recently but they would know, through the grapevine, what was happening or they could find out. Frank asked them to check on Gina and to help her if she needed it. He would repay them later, no matter what it took, no matter what it cost. They had his word on that. After some thought, he wrote a letter to Miller also, at the café. This letter was short and cautious. He made few claims on him, kept to the point. Gina seemed upset, were things okay and was there anything he could do to help? Not much more than that.

He handed the letters into the guardhouse that afternoon, praying that they would arrive quickly.

✳

She should have confronted him right away. She had caught him red-handed and she should have pressed home her advantage. He couldn't have denied it, not easily. She had seen him take the money and he would know that. That would have put her in control, given her the upper hand. There were other people around, too, which would have worked to her advantage. None of them could have seen him taking the money; he'd been too deft and careful for that. But they would know from the way he talked that he was guilty; he would be justifying himself too insistently, protesting his innocence too strenuously. They would see, in his eyes and in everything he did, that he had taken the money. All of this would have helped her. She could have dealt with the situation from a stronger position while he was, as it were, off-balance. But, of course, she had done none of this. Instead of challenging him while the ten-shilling note was still burning like a hot coal in his pocket, she drew back into the kitchen, away from the doorway.

In other words, Gina hesitated. And, in that one moment of perfectly understandable indecision, she was lost. That was the moment when Gina could still, relatively easily, have changed things; that was when she could have saved herself and Frank – and Miller, if you choose to look at it that way, too. But, by letting the moment pass, she gave up her last good chance to alter the course of things. There was, really, no turning back after that.

Of course, Gina couldn't see this at the time. The moment had slipped away long before she realised its significance. And when she finally did, it was too late to do anything about it. As she stood there, behind the door, Gina felt afraid more than anything else. She was suddenly more acutely aware than ever of being utterly alone and vulnerable. She'd lived in Paisley for about a year and a half. She spoke English reasonably well but she often couldn't understand the people who came into the café unless they made an effort to speak slowly. She couldn't, she was quite sure, run the café on her own. There were things she knew nothing about: dealing with the suppliers (most of whom were men), watching what was delivered, knowing what to reject and what to accept, knowing when there was better to be had and when there wasn't. She wasn't good at dealing directly with the customers, still slightly nervous of them, always straining to understand what they were saying. She knew nothing about hiring other staff or what to pay them. Miller had generally taken care of all that, kept it pretty much to himself. At first, Miller hadn't consciously tried to shut her out. It just made good sense for him to deal with certain things while she dealt with others. But, since the business of the embrace, she'd felt increasingly that he was actively excluding her at every possible opportunity. He was making it clear, both to her and the suppliers, that he would do the deals without reference to her. She could see this in the way the suppliers or their drivers looked past her if she answered the door and asked, 'Is Mr Miller around?' As far as they were concerned, Miller was the one who mattered, not her. She still needed him to keep the café open. She couldn't do it on her own.

As she waited behind the door, still trying to work out what to do, Gina was terrified that Miller would come walking into the kitchen at any second. If he did that – if he laid eyes on her at that moment – he would know that she had seen him take the money. She couldn't hide it from him. And this – a kind of guilt sprung from the fact that she hadn't acted – would make *her* seem like the one who had committed the crime.

Suddenly, right behind her, he banged a pile of plates down on a shelf and she jumped, feeling that he must know she was there. He came towards the doorway, his shoes clicking on the tiles in that particular rhythm of his; one heel striking the floor cleanly, the other making a more muted scuffing sound. But he stopped and turned away again, maybe just fetching cutlery from the box near the door. After another moment, she realised that he had gone out beyond the counter and she heard him talking to one of the customers. She couldn't make out what he was saying but he sounded relaxed and the conversation was regularly punctuated with small, familiar bursts of laughter. It almost sounded like the way things had been when Frank was out there. He always had that easy way with the customers, which Miller had only begun to acquire, almost as if mimicking Frank.

Yet again, not for the first time, nor the last, Gina wished that Frank was here. Right here, beside her, this moment. But he wasn't, of course, and she would have to deal with this herself. Frank would have spoken to him, she was sure of that; Frank would never have let it pass. So she would do the same, she would speak to him. But it would be better, she thought, to wait until the evening when the café was empty. That would give her time, too, to decide what to say.

Miller sensed fairly quickly that something had happened. Something had changed in her; it was as obvious as the weather outside the café windows. He couldn't say, though, with any certainty what had caused this. She couldn't have seen him take the money. She'd have said something. Surely she'd have said something. Perhaps she had known exactly how much was in the till before he lifted the ten bob note. Perhaps she'd been checking it when he wasn't around, though he hadn't seen any evidence of this. Nor had he seen her anywhere near the till. She was different, though; there was no mistaking that. She stayed in the back kitchen more than usual that afternoon, wouldn't meet his eyes even occasionally when their paths crossed. There was a tension in the air, and in her, that hadn't been there earlier. Maybe it had nothing to do with the money. Perhaps there had been word of Frank, but he would have known about that. She wouldn't have kept that to herself. Maybe she'd hurt herself, burned her hand on the cooker or cut herself. Maybe it was the time of month. Whatever it was, even if it was the money, he didn't care. He wasn't troubled in the least; she needed him too much.

At closing time, when the last customers left, he expected her to say something, to broach whatever was troubling her. But nothing happened. They simply started as usual on the regular nightly ritual of cleaning up, replacing stock, wiping down and laying the tables for tomorrow, each of them carrying out their own appointed tasks without regard to the other. They did all of this in silence, which was pretty much normal now. He thought that the silence tonight was perhaps a little deeper, more freighted, than usual but he could have been wrong. He was just keen to get out of here. Most nights now, on his way home, he would look into the Teagardens just up Causeyside Street for a game of dominos and a few drinks. He'd made friends in there with some of the regulars; good guys, he thought, though most people regarded them as wasters, chancers and shirkers. Miller enjoyed his couple of hours in the snug at the back of the bar when the day was ended. The time passed in a warm, whisky-coloured blur. It felt good to be part of a group, which wasn't something that had always come easily to Miller. He was definitely going to the Teagardens tonight, he decided; he'd earned himself a drink after today.

It was as he was heading towards the door, his coat on, work finished for the day, that she finally spoke. She was behind the counter, polishing and putting away the cutlery. All the lights in the café were off, to keep the wardens happy. The only light came from the open door of the kitchen and it fell softly onto her shoulders from behind, casting her face into shadow. She still wasn't sure, even after thinking about nothing else all afternoon and evening, how to handle this. But she couldn't let the moment pass.

'Can I have a word?' she heard herself saying. 'Before you go?'

'Sure,' he said, turning to face her. He wasn't in the least bothered, she could see that.

'Will it take long?' he asked. 'I've got friends tae meet.'

She looked down for a moment, folded the tea towel and laid it on the counter in front of her.

'No,' she said after a moment. 'No' long.'

What to say? What would Frank do here?

'I'm listening,' he said, when she still didn't break the silence.

'It's about the till.'

'What about the till?'

'I'm no' sure it's always been right recently.'

He was looking at her intently now, his eyes gleaming with the yellow light from the kitchen. He was enjoying this.

'How d'you mean?' he said, not moving, standing foursquare in front of her, his voice quiet and steady.

'I think it's been short a couple of days.'

'Just a couple?'

'It's hard to say.'

'Aye, it would be, wouldn't it?'

Maybe it would be enough to show him that she knew money was missing. Maybe that would make him stop.

'Yes, it would,' she said eventually. 'But I still think it's been short.'

She was going to insist on this, not move away from this fact. That was the least she could do.

'How much short?'

'I'm not sure.'

She'd seen something. She must have seen something. He thought he'd heard a rustling noise behind him as he took the money that afternoon. And he'd looked round because of it but the doorway had been empty. Angel's wings, he'd said to himself, joking. A guilty conscience – who would have believed it?

'Well, there's only you an' me in here.'

She nodded.

'Do you think I would take money from you? Or Frank?'

'No,' she said after a moment, shaking her head too vigorously. 'That's not what I'm saying.'

'This place wouldnae be open if it wasnae for me.'

'I know.'

'An' when Frank was here an' you were ill.'

'I know that, too. I'm sorry.'

He was safe; he knew that now. He still couldn't decide if she had seen him take the ten bob note that afternoon. The chances were, she probably had. But it didn't matter a damn. He had the upper hand here, he was in control.

'I don't understand what you're sayin' to me,' he said, taking a couple of steps forward and leaning one elbow on the counter. His voice carried a lingering trace of hurt at the implication but also managed to sound soothing and sympathetic.

'I don't know myself, I'm sorry.'

She couldn't go any further than she had already gone. She worried that she'd gone too far, made her meaning too clear. He didn't seem in the least intimidated or bothered. She was the one who felt uncomfortable. But maybe that was just her, maybe he was better at hiding what he was really feeling. She was clinging to the hope that the hint would be enough for him. That this would make him change his ways. Being basically a good person herself, Gina allowed for the existence of the same good in others, even in someone like Miller.

'Have you seen anybody take money from the till?' he asked with an odd sense of exhilaration, like someone on a high wire, confident that he couldn't fall.

'No,' she answered quietly, after a moment.

He shook his head, extending her sympathy.

'Maybe you're mistaken about the money.'

'We're definitely taking less some days. We're down on what we should be.' She wasn't going to back away from that.

'We're down on what we used to be,' he said, his voice almost a whisper. 'But the place isn't as busy as it used to be. Fewer people in. And they're not buying so much. More often just the cup of tea without the bun or the sandwich now. People are finding it tough.'

'That's true,' she said.

'Maybe that's all it is.'

'Maybe.'

She was agreeing with him in everything she said. But there was still a hint of dissent in her manner, a refusal to concede victory. He sensed this and re-deployed his forces, suddenly taking a new line of attack that took her completely by surprise.

'But it's always possible, you know, that someone is getting into the till.'

She looked at him, almost dazed, not sure where he was going with this. And she was struggling, as always, to keep up with his English and to form her own answers in this strange, difficult language.

'Maybe it's a supplier. Or one of the customers. Could be a kid, even. These kids are quick. I try to keep an eye on them, do my best, but you know what they're like.'

'Yes,' she said.

'Maybe it could be something like that.'

Miller smiled. He'd rarely experienced such a clear and unambiguous sense of power over another person in his life. He had a good time in the Teagardens when he finally got there that night, really tore into the whisky and bought a few rounds for everyone else. He'd done well, he thought, handled it just right. She wouldn't cause him any trouble, no trouble at all.

Gina slept badly that night, replaying the conversation over and over in her head. She wondered if she shouldn't have been more direct. But, in all honesty, she didn't see that she could have done anything else or dealt with the situation in any other way. She needed him and she hoped this talk would do the trick. He was a decent man; surely he would do the decent thing – for Frank, if not for her.

Within a few days, she realised that nothing had changed. She was sure money was still being taken. It was almost as if he was being more deliberate about it now, not caring whether she knew or not. And his manner towards her was harder, with no longer any trace of deference. He disregarded her more and more, treated her as if she wasn't there or she didn't matter. He chivvied her one night in no uncertain terms when she was slow bringing out a couple of fish suppers. And he kept on about this later, when the customers had gone and they were alone together, saying she'd need to be sharper. All of that was something he'd never done before. He'd never have dared.

⋆

The next letter arrived on the last Tuesday in November. It was a recent letter, posted at the beginning of November. The handwriting was shaky, the letters badly formed, the words meandering off their lines. He moved slightly away from the other men and tore the envelope open. The letter itself was just one page long and was as vague and repetitious as the previous one. She told him several times that she loved him and missed him. She was finding things more difficult than she'd expected, she wrote, but she didn't go into details. There were whole lines that were indecipherable. In other places, she'd written something and then crossed it out many times over. This letter was so completely different from the earlier letters that Frank had no doubt that something was wrong and she was hiding it from him.

Frank wondered briefly about asking Burke if he could see the commander. But he knew this was pointless. There were no grounds, compassionate or otherwise, for release or reclassification. Not one of the internees had succeeded in being released from the camp since they had arrived in August. One man's wife and daughter had been killed in a bombing raid in London and he had been refused any special consideration. In his own case, Frank couldn't even say what the problem was. When you boiled it down, it was just a feeling, an instinct. The soldiers would laugh at him if he tried to put that into words. So Frank wrote again to Gina and Ravezzi. He didn't try Miller this time. He couldn't have said why; it just wasn't something that he wanted to do at that moment.

Early in December, they had a run of bad nights with the old man. They moved him into different positions, laid him on his side with his knees pulled up slightly, propped him on the edge of the bed, almost cradling him in their arms. Nothing helped. Nothing gave him any real relief or made his breathing easier.

Neither Frank nor the boy slept much during those nights. But then that was true of the other internees in the house, too, even the sailors They could hear Carlo throughout the house, even down in the kitchen which was a half-basement two floors below. The sound worked its way through the walls and the timbers, permeated them, so that sometimes it felt like the house itself was struggling to breathe. There was no hiding from the sound, no escaping. When he was at his worst, he could be heard outside in the street, even if the waves were breaking spectacularly on the beach fifty or sixty yards away. It was a sound that Frank never forgot. It stayed in his mind, an aural memory as precise as any image. Whenever he heard someone on a bus or in the street with a touch of emphysema, he was suddenly back in that boarding-house bedroom trying to nurse Carlo through the night. He could hear the soft thump of his own shoes on the wooden floorboards, feel the icy dampness of the night air and see the distant glimmer of the sea outside the window. And he would experience, briefly, the same paralysing sense of helplessness.

On the night of the fifth of December, Carlo was worse than ever. He had been very weak most of the day and the straining for breath was almost constant. They were running low on oxygen but the oxygen wasn't making much difference now. Around midnight, something changed in the old man. Frank couldn't have said what it was but he sensed it as clearly as if someone else had just entered the room.

'I'm goin' for the doctor,' Frank said to the boy. 'You want someone else to come and sit wi' you?'

'No, I'm all right. Just go!'

Frank ran downstairs and opened the door of the house. He stepped onto the pavement and shouted to the soldier on guard.

'We need the doctor for the old man.'

'Okay, okay. I can hear him from here.'

When Frank hurried back up the stairs, he found the other internees in the house had come out of their rooms. Some of them were standing on the stairs and several were on the top landing, outside the room where Carlo lay. They stayed near the doorway, reluctant to enter. One or two offered to help but everyone knew that there was nothing any of them could do now.

The doctor frowned slightly as he stepped into the room, sizing Carlo up, registering almost instantly what he was dealing with.

'It would be best,' he said to Frank as he sat on the edge of the bed and opened his bag, 'if we could have fewer people. Just you and the boy, that's all.'

The others were already turning away, slipping into the darkness, shuffling downstairs.

'You sure you want to stay?' Frank asked Josef, who was sitting on his own bed, white-faced, watching them intently. The boy nodded.

The doctor listened to Carlo's heart and chest, moving the stethoscope lightly but precisely around the old man's ribcage. It seemed to Frank that the doctor was looking for something that he couldn't find. He gave Carlo an injection, listened again to his breathing and gave him a second injection from a different phial. He placed a mask over Carlo's mouth and sprayed something into the mask from a bottle. 'To open his airways a bit,' he said. This brought Carlo some relief but he was barely conscious now and his breathing was so shallow it seemed at times to have stopped completely. After a while, the doctor looked at Frank from under his eyebrows and, ever so slightly, shook his head. The boy started to cry.

'I'm sorry,' said the doctor.

Frank nodded, knowing that there was nothing any doctor, or anyone else, could do for the old man now.

'I can wait,' said the doctor.

'We'll manage.'

The doctor put his hand on Frank's shoulder. He went over to the boy on his way out. He stopped in front of him as if about to say something. But, in the end, he said nothing and left.

The old man was at least quiet now, truly peaceful for the first time in days. The boy, who had stopped crying now, brought a chair over to the bed and sat beside him. Frank stood by the window, looking out at the sea and turning, every so often, to check the old man. He died just after four o'clock in the morning. Simply stopped breathing. As peacefully and quietly as if he was closing a book he'd just that minute finished.

The undertaker didn't come for the body until the afternoon. The boy wouldn't leave him, still crying from time to time. So Frank stayed with them. The other internees brought up food and cups of tea. The boy would neither eat nor drink.

They were not permitted to attend the old man's funeral. It was felt that this might cause unrest among the internees, unsettle them and lead to a disturbance of some kind. Long afterwards, when he was home, Frank could understand this. And he even agreed with the decision up to a point. But, at the time, it made him angry. Truly angry for perhaps the first time in his life.

★

It was around this time, in the last few weeks of November, that Gina began to withdraw more and more into herself. She hardly ever worked at the counter now, preferring to stay in the kitchen, avoiding both Miller and the customers. She wasn't going to chapel either, unwilling to tell the priest, even in confession, what had happened with Miller. She was still, in a sense, trying to deny it and was convinced that she was, somehow, partly to blame. Much later on, when people learned what had happened, they wondered at Gina's silence. Why didn't she speak to someone, they would ask. Why didn't she tell someone what was happening? All of this is easy to say with the benefit of hindsight. For Gina, at the time, it seemed that she had no real alternative. She was uncertain and confused, paralysed by fear. She was ashamed, too, appalled at the idea of telling anyone about the attempted embrace. Most of all, though, she wanted to keep the café going for Frank and, in order to do that, she believed that she needed Miller.

Also, it has to be said that Miller was astute and careful in the way he exploited the situation. One afternoon, for instance, Robert Glen looked into the café. He hadn't been around for weeks, was now working out of a station in Cardonald. She thought about saying something to Robert, wondered if she should ask to see him at the station. But almost as soon as he appeared, Miller turned up, working just behind her at the counter, able to hear every word. Robert had said to her, 'Well, you're lucky you had Ian here to help you, eh?'

And she had answered – had no option but to answer – 'Aye. Very lucky.'

And then Robert spoke to Miller for a while, man to man as it were. Watching them talk, Gina knew that she couldn't go to Robert now. She would seem hysterical, crazy. And Robert almost certainly would be inclined not to believe her. She'd just told him herself, with no apparent coercion, that she was lucky to have Miller around.

As she spent more time out of sight, in the back, Miller became increasingly the public face of the café. Customers who hadn't been in before, and who didn't know him, would assume he was the owner. If they caught a glimpse of Gina in the kitchen, they might assume that she was the hired help, a skivvy. It was around this time that Miller started dressing a little better: dark blue serge suits and white shirts with hard, gleaming paper collars which he changed every day. The money, of course, was no problem. If he needed something special, he'd just take a little more from the till, always trying not to be too reckless, of course. Though there was no real need to bother as she hardly ever came out into the café now.

On the first Saturday night in December, they were at their busiest, every table and every seat in the place taken. There were two extra waitresses working but neither of them women Gina knew, both having been hired in by Miller. There was a banging of plates and a constant buzz of noises and voices. People were moving around and there was a small queue of people waiting at the door for tables. Gina had come out briefly to collect the dirty plates. She was briskly gathering up the cutlery and stacking the plates. Miller came right up behind her and rang up 5s 6d on the till for two fish suppers and teas. He seemed to think that, because she had her back to him, she couldn't see him. Or perhaps he didn't care. But the mirror gave her a clear view right down into the shiny black interior of the cash drawer. And she could see quite clearly that he dropped only a few pennies into the cash register. There was no glint of silver.

She didn't say anything at the time; the moment was over so

quickly and he was back out, weaving his way between the tables to take another order, before she realised quite what she'd seen. But that night, after the last customers and the waitresses had gone, she turned from the sink where she was drying glasses as he came back in from the yard, having just taken out two jingling, rattling cases of empty lemonade bottles. It was after eight o'clock, pitch black outside. She said, 'I saw you taking money today.'

He stopped and looked at her for a long moment. Then he shook his head and started to move on, continuing on his way out to the café. There was a faint smile on his lips. He wasn't even going to deny it or try to defend himself. It was almost as if she hadn't spoken, as if she wasn't there.

'You rang up 5s 6d. But you only put some coppers in the till.'

He shook his head.

'I saw you. In the mirror.'

Now he stopped, leaning over to one side in the doorway.

'No, you must have made a mistake,' he said, still smiling. He'd been waiting for this. Was surprised that she hadn't said something before this. But he wasn't bothered or worried. There was nothing, he felt quite sure, that she could do to him.

'I've seen you before.'

He raised his eyebrows in mock surprise.

'Why didn't you say somethin'? Why didn't you say somethin' this afternoon?'

'I didn't want a fuss.'

'If I saw someone taking money from me, I wouldnae care about that. I'd make a fuss.'

'There were customers here,' she said, already – to her own surprise – on the defensive.

'I wouldnae care about that, either.'

He was wary of her but he wasn't frightened. He felt strangely safe here, unthreatened, almost in a state of grace. Maybe it was a good thing that she'd brought this up. Maybe the air needed clearing.

'I know what I saw.'

He shrugged, clearly not caring either way.

'Lot of people wouldnae believe you. They'd say maybe you were just imaginin' it. Neurotic lonely woman, lot of worries.'

'You stole money.'

'Only your word for that,' he said. 'An' if you didnae mention it at the time, then people would wonder – did she really see that? Maybe just her imagination workin' overtime.'

She had expected him to be surprised, maybe even to apologise. She hadn't expected this utter lack of shame and this defiance. It almost felt as if the tables had been turned and she was the one in the wrong. That he was the innocent party and she was the guilty one, the one making wild and false accusations.

'I saw you with my own eyes. I've seen you take money other times, too.'

'And you never mentioned that either?'

She didn't answer. She wasn't going to play this game.

'See, lots of people would find that hard to believe.'

'I know what I saw,' she repeated.

He shrugged and leaned back against the table, almost sitting on it. It was raining outside. They could hear cars hissing past on the road. Someone ran towards the café, footsteps slapping and splashing in the rain. For one crazy moment, she thought it was Frank. Then the footsteps continued on past the café, dying away into silence.

'Fire me,' he said.

'What?' she said, not really understanding this, the language yet again just escaping her.

'If you think I took something that didnae belong to me, you should fire me. That's what I'd do in your shoes.'

The silence made her dizzy. She felt as if the air was being drawn out of the tiny room and it was becoming difficult to breathe. The walls were closing in on her. She was shaking. She could see her hands trembling in front of her. He could see this, too.

'What you going to do?'

He was grinning. She didn't know what to answer.

'Maybe you don't know what you saw, after all.'

'I know.'

'So why don't you fire me?'

She leaned against the sink, afraid that she would fall.

'You can't get rid of me, can you?'

He pushed himself up from the table and came towards her, moving quickly, the limp barely perceptible.

'Can't run your precious café without me.'

He turned slightly and looked around, surveying the place almost as if it were his own.

'You need me to run this place. You could never do it on your own. And you want it to be here when Frank comes back. Don't you?'

She stared at him, unable to speak. Now she was terrified of him. This wasn't what should have happened. This wasn't how she should have handled it.

'Don't you?' he screamed at her.

'Yes, I do. I really do.'

He was leaning towards her, just a few feet away. Looking right into her eyes.

'There wouldnae be any café if it werenae for me.'

'I know.'

And he cast up again the time she had been ill. And he had run the café by himself.

'I know all that, too,' she said, almost in tears, but trying to fight them back, knowing they would put her at even more of a disadvantage here.

'So why you havin' a go at me?' he yelled at her, his spit landing on her face. 'Eh? What makes you think you can have a go at me?'

He was angry now, redness flushing in the skin around his neck, his eyes glinting at her, no longer so much in control.

'You never did this before. When Frank was here,' she said, her voice barely a whisper.

'Maybe I should have done. Fuckin' wonderful Frank. Frank this, Frank that. I'm sick to here wi' Frank. It's no' him that's kept this place goin' an' you fed. It's me. Me!'

'Don't shout. Please.'

'I helped Frank more than he ever helped me,' he screamed down at her, his face just inches from hers. He was rewriting history in his mind now. He believed this totally, utterly. Without any doubt, that was how it had been.

'Best thing that ever happened to Frank when I turned up here.'

She was shaking her head, no longer making any attempt to hide her tears.

He grabbed her by the wrists, hard. And he forced her to look at him.

'I just want what's mine. You understand that?'

'It's no' right.'

'Aye, it is.'

'When Frank comes back –'

'We'll worry about that when it happens.'

'Let me go. You're hurting.'

'I'll take what's owed to me when I like. That clear?'

She shook her head, turning away from him.

'Is that clear?'

He jerked her back towards him, moving her easily. She had no strength in her body, nothing compared to his strength.

'And if you tell anyone, I'll walk out of here. I'll make sure none of the suppliers come anywhere near you. I'll let the bank know that you've no money. The manager trusts me. He knows what's what here. He knows who's keeping this place runnin'.'

She was still trying to free herself. He jerked her wrists again, making her yelp. This time, she came crashing towards him. And he felt her body pressed against his; her breasts, her hips, the small provocative bump of her pubic bone. He could smell her skin; soap and a hint of perfume, something floral, a scent that caught at the back of his throat. And before he knew it, he was drawing her down to the cold stone floor of the kitchen, using the weight of his body to pin her there, tearing at her clothes.

6

The first letter from old man Ravezzi came before Christmas. Even after he'd read it several times, Frank still wasn't sure what to make of it.

He had been lucky, the old man wrote, dealing with himself first before he came on to other matters. The local police had turned a blind eye when they were told to arrest him. He'd closed the café, though. There had been some trouble early in the summer and, besides, he couldn't cope with the work now, not without his sons. The craziness of internment had seen them being despatched halfway across the world to Australia. 'God knows when we'll ever see them again,' he wrote. But the boys were okay; they'd had a letter with a photograph. They said Australia was fine, there was plenty of food and they were being well looked after. Old man Ravezzi wrote that he missed the café. It had been his life and he was lost without it, never really knowing what to do with himself. He forced himself to walk along the Esplanade every day, to the Cloch lighthouse and back – as long as the wind wasn't blowing him off his feet, he wrote.

He didn't say much about Gina. He hadn't been up to Paisley himself but he'd phoned around. People told him that the café was doing well. Miller was still there, working hard by all accounts. But folk didn't see a lot of Gina. She stayed in the kitchen more now as far as he could make out, taking care of the food. She didn't leave the café very often now, it seemed. Someone had spoken to her briefly at early morning mass a few weeks back but no one had seen her since. She was probably just keeping herself to herself, which was sensible in the circumstances. 'It's the war,' he wrote. 'It's turned everything on its head. Don't worry. I'm sure things will be fine when you come back home.'

This was the part of the letter that Frank kept thinking about – 'I'm sure things will be fine when you come back home.' What did that mean? Did it mean that things weren't 'fine' now? Why hadn't he spoken to Gina herself? He could easily have phoned the café and spoken to her directly. Had he even tried to do that? It didn't sound as if he had. And if not, why not? It was good to have the letter. But the truth was it didn't set Frank's mind at ease. There was something tentative about it, something lingering in the shadows there which he could only sense but not distinguish with any accuracy. Or was he simply imagining all of this? He knew that was more than possible. They were coming up to Christmas and that made life difficult for all of the internees. People were edgier, less forgiving, more short-tempered. There had been more than the usual number of arguments and sudden outbursts of anger and frustration, sometimes breaking into scuffles and fights, rarely for any very good reason. Frank and the boy were as affected by this mood as everyone else. And the old man's death was still very much on their minds. His suitcase lay under his bed by the window, containing everything he'd brought with him. Frank had no idea what they would do with this. But he couldn't throw it away. No man's life, he felt, should be that disposable or mean so little. In the end, of course, someone else took or discarded the case and it was lost like a pebble dropped in the river. It certainly never found its way back, as Frank had hoped, to Carlo's family.

It was a curious time, that Christmas. They were, on the whole, warm and comfortable, even if that meant taking to your bed for the day while you were wearing your suit and overcoat. They were well-fed, more so than lots of people on the mainland, as the soldiers constantly reminded them. The soldiers generally treated them decently, though there was, inevitably, the odd bad apple. They weren't constantly being moved and forced to sleep and eat wherever they found themselves. So their life now was, on the surface, better than it had been in those early weeks of anxiety, fear and uncertainty. But that time either side of Christmas brought its own problems. The pressure of wondering what would happen to you was replaced by the pressure of wondering what you would do for the next few minutes or the next few minutes after that. And you tried not to think what you might do for the next few hours or the next day. Time dragged its feet with a vengeance. There was nothing to do except sit around and get on each other's nerves. And if you had worries or problems back home – and Frank was far from alone in this – then you had all the time you needed to drive yourself half-mad trying to explain and understand things that you would never explain or understand until you went home and saw the truth for yourself.

People tried, where they could, to find diversions, ways of cheating time. The sailors in the house had discovered how to steal beer from the quartermaster's stores. On the nights they managed this, they took over the kitchen, drank, sang, sometimes shouted and argued until the beer was finished. Occasionally, they'd use rubber hoses to pass gas through the beer and turn it into a truly lethal concoction. When they drank this, the night invariably ended with a fight or a beating. There was nothing half-hearted about these beatings, either; there were broken arms and legs and people ended up in the hospital for weeks at a time. The soldiers knew what was happening but they wouldn't risk coming into the house with the sailors drunk and fired up. On those nights, Frank kept the boy in their room. If they needed something from the kitchen, Frank would fetch it. If the boy had to use the toilet on the landing, Frank would stand outside the door until he had finished. Sometimes Marek appeared in the kitchen. He was, as far as Frank could make out, involved in procuring the beer. He stayed in the kitchen and kept out of their way. But there was no doubt, from his manner, that he had never forgotten the boxing match. And never would.

Josef had found a diversion of his own in the run-up to Christmas. One night, he came into their room very late and woke Frank.

'Look what I've got,' he said and opened the pouch of his jumper to reveal half a dozen red apples, the rain still gleaming on their skins.

'Where-a did ye get those?' said Frank.

'Ah, there's the thing,' said Josef, his soft words underlining the fact that, as he was picking up English, he was also picking up Frank's Scottish accent. He and a couple of other young internees had found a way of slipping out of the camp. These expeditions were modest affairs. They rarely went far and tended to stay within the gardens of the houses nearby. The apples had come from a garden shed where the autumn crop had been laid on newspapers over slats of wood for the winter. Most nights, when they went out, Josef would return with some little souvenir. Sometimes it was an old newspaper. Another time, it was a set of picture postcards of Douglas and the Isle of Man which he stuck up on the wall above his bed. Sometimes, it was a bottle of milk or fresh butter lifted from an outside larder.

The boy so evidently wanted to please Frank with these trophies, which he invariably drew, with a magician-like flourish, from his pockets or the inside of his jumper. And Frank was always suitably impressed and grateful. He took pleasure, too, in simply hearing what the boy had seen: the couple kissing in the doorway, the family listening to the radio while they played cards on the kitchen table, the (heavily depleted) brass band practising in the church hall. These surreptitious, second-hand glimpses of the ordinary world were reassuring. They reminded him that, beyond the fence, life still went on pretty much as normal for most people despite the war. And they seemed to promise that his and Gina's life would, at some point, also return to normal.

*

When he had finished, they lay on the kitchen floor for what seemed to her like hours but could only have been seconds. Time had slipped its moorings, was no longer anchored in the rock, something fixed and precise. Nothing was the same as before, nothing could be the same. The world had shattered around them and the fragments of their previous life were turning and shifting in the void like shards of glass.

At first Gina, still frozen with shock, was unable to move, trapped by his weight. Eventually, he moved slightly and this enabled her to squirm out from under him. She half-crawled across the kitchen, sobbing, clutching at her clothes, vainly trying to pull them around her, and stumbled through the doorway that led to the flat upstairs.

He lay on the floor for a while longer. Then he dragged himself up and switched off the light, wishing that the light had been off earlier. He wished, too, that he could switch off the light in his memory but that was something he'd never be able to do.

He went out to the yard at the back of the café and looked up at the windows of the flat. No lights. He lit a cigarette and drew it to his lips, his hands shaking so that the red tip of the cigarette danced in the darkness. There had been no single moment when he made the decision to cross that particular threshold. This whole thing had happened almost without him, despite him. He felt merely like a disinterested spectator, a bystander. He could remember next to nothing about what he had felt while it was actually happening. Certainly, there had been no pleasure in it. Nothing remotely like pleasure.

He was appalled and terrified. He let the cigarette drop from his fingers and heard it sizzle briefly in one of the shallow puddles that gleamed like silver on the paving stones. He was waiting for the blow that must surely land, as if retribution was now inevitable. He had no idea where the blow would come from, or what form it would take. But land it would, and soon. Of that he was utterly convinced.

Slowly, over the next hour or so, while he stood there in the courtyard and she remained upstairs in the flat, he began to regain control of himself. There was no need to be afraid, he told himself. There was no blow to fear, no inevitable retribution. This was all there was; this cold yard and him and her. He could find a way through this, he told himself. He could deal with this, if he was sensible and careful. He had to stop her from telling anyone, that was the main thing. Keep it between the two of them. Persuade her that this would be best for everyone: for her, for him, most of all for Frank.

Someone rattled the front door of the café, startling him. He looked at his watch: ten past ten. Robert Glen, most likely. Thank God he had switched off the light. But it was still relatively early; Robert would expect them to be here. What would she do? Would she even have heard the knock? It had made him jump, like a gunshot, but it hadn't actually been that loud, might not have carried upstairs. He couldn't hear anything from up there. No footsteps. No movement of any sort. There was a second rap on the glass.

Still nothing from upstairs.

Then, after a few minutes, everything was silent again. Robert, if it had been Robert, had given up and gone away. What should he do? What would she do? There was no phone up there so she couldn't call anyone. And she hadn't come down. But he should be more careful, keep a closer eye on her. He went back into the kitchen, determined to make sure that she didn't go out. He kept the light off. Didn't want to encourage any more visitors.

He spent the whole night there, sitting beside the kitchen table, in front of the door to the upstairs flat. Around six, the deliveries started arriving. The drivers knocked on the back door. He didn't answer, not wanting any of them to see him unshaven, clearly having spent the night here. Most of them, when they didn't get an answer, left their trays of loaves and rolls and crates of milk or vegetables in the yard. Gina and Miller could be trusted; they would sign for the supplies later. At first, he worried that all of this activity would bring her downstairs. Then later, when the first customers started trying the door around eight thirty, he worried why she hadn't come down. He couldn't open the café, looking as he did. And he couldn't leave to change or clean himself up until he had spoken to her. Soon after nine, he decided that he couldn't wait any longer. He would go up and see her.

She had washed herself in the bath when she went upstairs. Then she had crawled into bed, still wet. She was barely aware of the passage of time. She would drift off into a shallow, troubled sleep for a few minutes and then wake with a start. Each time she woke, she remembered what had happened and it was as if it was happening again, as painful and shaming as the first time. She knew that she should do something, tell someone. But she couldn't bear to move, couldn't bear to think about what had happened, never mind tell someone else about it. Could she even find the words in English to describe it? And who would she tell: the police? the priest? She couldn't do that, didn't see how she could even begin to do that. And she wondered too if it had somehow been her fault. Had she done something to cause it? Had she somehow – without knowing it – provoked him? She kept thinking: if her sister had been here . . . if Frank had been here . . . But neither of them was here. It was only her and Miller. She was quite sure that he was downstairs, that he had stayed there all night. There were no lights showing under the front door of the flat. But she knew that he was there like one animal sensing another. She had never felt so alone in her life. She had prayed to God, asked Him for help and guidance. But there was no sense – not even the slightest hint – of anyone or anything reaching out to her. Nothing cut through the confusion and fear and uncertainty.

When she heard him at the door, she was terrified. He tried the handle, which was locked, of course. He didn't bother knocking. He put his shoulder to the lock several times and burst it open. She moved to the top of the bed, terrified, drawing the bedclothes around her as if they would offer some kind of protection. He looked in the other rooms but came quickly into the bedroom.

'I just want to talk to you,' he said.

He took a few steps into the room but stopped at the foot of the bed. It would be best, he told her, if they didn't say anything about last night. Why would she want anyone else to know? It was better if it was just them, their secret. What good would it do for the whole town to know? What good would it do Frank? He would hear about it in his camp. Someone would be sure to write and tell him. How would he feel hearing it like that? Even if she did go to the police or anyone else, how could she be sure they would believe her? He could easily say that she had wanted it. That it wasn't the first time. That it had been her who started it. How could she prove otherwise? When you came down to it, it was just her word against his. Plenty of people thought they were having it off already. Plenty of people thought they'd been doing that for months. She kept shaking her head and pulling the bedclothes tightly around her. She couldn't concentrate on what he was saying. She wanted him to stop, that was all that was in her mind. Eventually there was silence in the room but she couldn't remember him going, hadn't actually registered the moment when he left her alone and went back downstairs.

He was going to be okay, he told himself. He had nothing

to fear from her. Miller was almost certain of this as he came back down into the kitchen and heard someone else rattling the handle on the front door. If she was going to tell anyone, she'd have done it already. Even if she did it now, it would go against her. Why had she waited so long to complain, they would say. Why didn't you come to us right away, as soon as it happened? No, she wasn't going to be any trouble. He could relax a little now, for the first time since last night.

He slipped out the back door and hurried home, managing not to meet anyone that he knew on the way. He washed, shaved and changed his clothes. Then he went back to the café. She was still upstairs, hadn't gone anywhere. He felt quite safe now. Having washed and changed, he could even deny that the whole thing had happened. She couldn't prove anything, even if she tried. All he had to do was carry on as normal. The sooner he had the place open, the better for him. He set about bringing in the deliveries, unpacking the vegetables and the bread and rolls, putting them where they would be needed later. He opened the front door and quickly swept the floor. He cleared the tables that were still dirty from last night and had the place more or less ship-shape before the first couple of customers came in looking for tea and cakes.

He managed on his own that morning, keeping the menu simple and telling people that Gina had a bad cold. He waited to see if she would come down. But when she hadn't appeared by twelve he called one of the women who helped out and between them they managed pretty well for the rest of the day. The woman asked if she could go up and see Gina but Miller said she wanted to be left alone, didn't want to pass her cold onto anyone else.

That night, Miller cleared up by himself. He wondered about going up to see her again but decided, finally, against it. Leave her, he thought. Let her be. He had nothing really to fear from her now. He locked up as usual that night and went straight home, deciding that it would be better to give the bar a miss for a few nights at least.

When he came back in the morning, she was still upstairs. She hadn't been out, hadn't even come downstairs as far as he could judge. He had brought a new lock for the door of the flat. He didn't want anyone to see that it had been broken. So the first thing he did that morning was to replace it and repair, as best he could, the wood round about it. When he had finished, he called out to her. He had decided that he wouldn't go into the flat, that he would just leave her alone. But she didn't answer and this bothered him and then worried him. What if she wasn't here? He looked in the living room and the kitchen. No sign of her. No sign of anyone having been here. He pushed open the bedroom door. She was still in bed.

'You no' hear me?'

She didn't answer. He could see her hand trembling slightly.

'I've changed the lock. It was broke,' he said.

She still didn't move or respond in any way. He put the new key on the sideboard.

'There's your key.'

He had, of course, kept a copy for himself.

'You should come downstairs.'

She shook her head.

'It would be better for you.'

'No.'

This was said quietly but there was a note of defiance in her voice that stopped him as he was turning to the door.

'You'll need to learn to do what I say.'

She turned her head away, as if dismissing him. He came quickly back towards her and dragged her across the bed towards him, stifling her cries with his hand over her mouth even though there was no one downstairs to hear.

✶

In the weeks after Christmas, they began to see Marek in the house more frequently. He hadn't moved back in. But he was there regularly during the day and nearly always at night. His return to favour was mainly due to his ability to steal beer from the quartermaster's stores. The word in the camp was that he bribed some of the soldiers to allow him access to the stores. No one knew this for certain. But it was hard to see how he could have stolen so much for so long otherwise.

How he managed it, of course, was of no interest to Frank. What did matter was that he was a fixture in the house again, skulking around, staring at Frank and Josef whenever they were anywhere in sight. Frank warned the boy to keep clear of Marek and not to allow himself to be provoked. And he tried to believe in Josef's promises that he would be careful and avoid any confrontations. But the boy was only human and Frank knew better than to place too much confidence in the boy's vehement assurances.

They had to move. Something would happen if they stayed. That was as certain as if it were written in stone. Ideally, they should move to another camp. But another house would suffice for the time being. When he asked Burke about this, the sergeant simply laughed at him. If he could find another room here, fine. But the camp was already overcrowded. The other camps were much the same. And he was far too busy to spend time on something as trivial as this. Frank tried to make Burke see the danger that he could see and feel every day. Burke said that once things settled he'd move them but they'd have to make the best of it for now. When Frank tried to restate his case yet again, Burke said he'd heard all he wanted to hear about this. '*All*,' he said with emphasis, as Frank started to speak again.

Frank had already looked for a room in one of the other houses. Every room was taken and in some of them men were sleeping on mattresses on the floor. He told Josef that he should move in with one of his friends. Josef refused. That would be too obvious, he said. It would be like running away. And if he was still in the camp, then he wouldn't be running very far. He wasn't afraid, he said. And Frank nodded and said that was what he was afraid of.

Later, Frank blamed himself for giving up too easily. He should have insisted on the boy moving in with his friend. He should have spoken to the doctor or the chaplain. He should have made a better case when he was talking to Burke. He shouldn't have accepted the boy's promises that he would stay out of trouble. But Frank had worries of his own at the time. He had received just one letter in the whole of January. It was an old letter of Gina's, written early in the summer. So his thoughts were constantly on her and what might be happening in the café. It was nothing less than an obsession. He could tell himself to stop dwelling on Gina and the café, that it was fruitless and a waste of time. But he couldn't actually stop himself from doing it. The puzzle of what had happened, of what had changed in her life to provoke such a change in her letters, touched him too deeply. It infected his thoughts like a malevolent virus. He turned the puzzle over in his mind at all times of the day and night. He conjured up an endless series of scenarios to explain the facts he knew. None of these imagined solutions satisfied him for long. And, of course, none came close to the terrible truth. But even if Frank hadn't been so preoccupied, it's doubtful whether he could have really helped the boy. Given the fact that they were trapped there, living on top of each other, during those dark days early in 1941, it's hard to see how things could have turned out differently – no matter what Frank or anyone else had done.

In the camp, much of their life was routine. They cooked and ate their meals at roughly the same time every day, a strict rota being the only way so many men could use one small kitchen. They cleaned their room and made their beds after breakfast every morning. They had their days for washing. They usually went together to the guard house at eleven to see if Frank had a letter. One of their many rituals was that every morning, after they'd swept out the room and made the beds, Josef would fill up a large enamel jug in the kitchen. They used this for drinking from throughout the day and during the night. There was a bathroom on their floor, just across the landing from their room, but the water there came from a tank in the loft and wasn't mains. Josef had found this jug in his early days of scavenging and it had come in useful when Carlo had been ill. They would give him sips of water to help him with the coughing. And sometimes they'd pour it into a basin and use it to bathe his face when he was feverish. They didn't much talk about Carlo's death but Frank was aware that it had affected both of them deeply. For the boy, the jug was a connection to

Carlo. Frank knew that, odd as it might seem, this task of filling the jug was one of the ways in which the boy memorialised the old man. With most other things, they split their responsibilities fairly down the middle. But Frank was happy to leave the jug to the boy.

One day, early in February, Josef took the jug down to the kitchen. It was around ten, his usual time for doing this; in other words, after they'd cleaned the room and before they'd checked if Frank had any letters. Marek was sitting at the kitchen table with three or four other sailors. This wasn't unusual. And he paid no particular attention to Josef when he came into the kitchen.

Josef washed the plates he'd brought down, then emptied out the last of the old water from the jug and gave it a rinse. He let the tap run for a few moments and refilled the jug. The jug was white with a blue line round the middle and along either side of the handle. It had a lid which you lifted by pressing down your thumb on the lever and which usually closed again with a quiet 'clang'. When he was standing at the sink, he noticed that a couple of Frank's shirts had come off the line. They were lying over the scrawny bushes in the back border. Josef went down the short flight of stairs into the garden, retrieved the shirts and hung them back up on the line. It was a good drying day, some sun and a steady strong wind.

Back in the kitchen he lifted the jug and the plates. As he was stepping out of the door into the hall, he heard Marek laugh. The other men echoed this. Josef told himself to ignore it, they could be laughing at anything.

In the room, he put the jug in its usual place on the small table beside Carlo's bed. Frank was in the bathroom across the landing, washing socks. He had the door open and was talking to Josef.

Josef picked up a comic and was looking through it. He'd found comics useful for improving his English. And he enjoyed them. He went over to the window and sat down on the chair beside Carlo's bed. He looked out of the window and noticed that Marek and the sailors had moved outside. They were sitting on the low wall in front of the house. Marek was looking directly up at him and smiling.

After a moment, Josef turned to the jug. He lifted the lid and saw the turd floating in the water. He closed his eyes and cursed. Then he picked up the jug and charged out of the room. Frank was still talking across the landing to him. He'd heard about a room that might be available in another house and said maybe they could go and look at it. He didn't realise what had happened. It was only after a moment that he looked out of the bathroom and saw their room was empty.

He dried his hands on his trousers as he rushed with increasing urgency downstairs. In the hall, bodies blocked his way to the doorway. There was shouting from the street and the hurrying scuffle of feet. Frank pushed and said that they had to let him through. But they didn't move. The captain was at the door, looking out. Frank struggled and kicked, trying to force his way through. The shouting from outside was louder and more frenzied. Excited, in some sick way. He saw the captain look back and smile at him. He shouted at them and cursed. But still no one moved. The sailors were holding him there so that he could neither go forward nor move back and look for another way out of the house.

This and the shouting continued for a good few moments. He

heard a soldier's whistle. But the shouting virtually drowned it out. Frank was punching at the bodies around him, determined to reach the doorway.

Then, quite suddenly, the shouting stopped and Frank could hear the seagulls crying and the waves breaking distantly on the shore. The bodies around him were peeling away. No one was impeding him now. His way to the door was clear.

As he stepped out into the light, men were dispersing, moving quickly away from the front of the house. Soldiers were running along the street towards them, waving their rifles and blowing their whistles. At the foot of the steps, Marek was lying on his side, half on the pavement and half on the road. Josef was standing over him. He held Marek's knife in his hand, an ordinary kitchen knife sharpened to a point and with insulating tape wrapped round the handle. He was looking up at Frank and shaking his head.

*

Miller let Gina stay upstairs, a ghost in the attic, for a week or so. But he knew people were talking. And it was this, as much as anything, that prompted him to act.

Early one morning in the second week, he went upstairs to see her. She was terrified and edged away, keeping her distance from him. He told her that she had to come downstairs and start working. No, she cried, she couldn't do that. She couldn't face anybody. He shouted at her, threatened her, eventually grabbed her and physically dragged her downstairs into the kitchen. She refused to do anything. She was crying, hysterical.

After a moment or so, he decided to try another tack. He would tell people, he said, that she had slept with him, that she had pleaded with him to sleep with her. He would make sure everyone in the town knew. No doubt Frank would get to hear sooner or later. Was that what she wanted?

That morning, when the other women arrived, they were surprised to find her in the kitchen, baking scones. They could see that she was different, that something had happened. But Miller had already prepared the ground for this, hinting over the last few days at some kind of breakdown brought on by the business with Frank. This version of events rippled out from the café, as these things do, and soon became the accepted, unquestioned reason for Gina's increasingly strange and withdrawn behaviour. People were concerned for Gina and were sympathetic towards her situation. But people also discovered a certain warmth and respect for Miller himself, which had never been the case before. He was going out of his way to help Gina when, strictly speaking, there was no need. He could easily walk away from all of this. And yet he chose to stay and see it through. Of course, the truth eventually found its way out but not until much later. And even then no one could prove anything. Miller had managed it as well as anyone could have done.

It was around this time that Miller had Gina sign some papers. She barely knew what she was doing, couldn't understand them. But these papers gave him access to the bank account, making him an equal partner in the business with her and Frank. No one knew anything about this at the time. Miller was careful to keep this very quiet. He used a solicitor called Harry Pollock who was struck off a couple of years after the war ended for stealing money from clients. People said later that the bank manager, a friend of Pollock's, was in on this too. But there was no way of proving it. Certainly, at the time, no one suspected any of them.

As far as the town was concerned, Gina and Frank still owned the café. And Miller, despite what people had thought of him previously, was turning out to be something of a saint.

As they moved through Christmas and into 1941, a new pattern established itself in the café. Miller now decided everything. He looked after the money, paid the bills and the wages, chose whom to hire and not hire. He had an ease about him now and somehow the limp seemed to be less obvious though it was, in fact, exactly as it had always been. He ran the café from in front of the counter just as Frank used to do. He welcomed people in, sat them at their seats, snapped his fingers to call over a waitress. He drew up the bills and no one else was allowed near the cash register. He hardly ever did any lifting or carrying now. He brought in two young boys to do that; one for the early mornings and one to clear up at night. Gina was just a shadowy presence in the kitchen. Few customers ever saw her now and hardly any of them asked after her. Robert Glen had observed this change and took most people's view of it; Gina had had a breakdown and was lucky to have Miller around. Without him, the café would have closed and there would be no money coming in. No one really doubted this story because there was little reason to do so. Gina's spirit had clearly been broken, everyone could see that. But no one knew what had broken it or could begin to fathom Gina's isolation and overwhelming, paralysing sense of shame.

Old man Ravezzi came up from Gourock one day to see for himself what was happening. Miller was worried when he saw him stamping through the doorway. He wondered if the old man would somehow get through to her. Would she break down? What would she tell him? And they would talk in Italian so he wouldn't understand a word. He was trying to decide how to handle this, how to keep the upper hand, when he suddenly heard the door to the upstairs flat closing.

As soon as Gina saw the old man in the café, she panicked and ran upstairs. She was terrified that he would somehow sense her shame. She was sure that she couldn't hide it from him. Miller followed her upstairs and talked to her for a few minutes. When he went back down, he shrugged his shoulders and told Ravezzi that she wouldn't come down. Miller was sorry about this, he said, but this was how she had been for some time now. Old man Ravezzi had, of course, heard something about Gina's withdrawal from things. He was upset to see that it was true; worse than he had thought, if anything.

Miller and Ravezzi sat at one of the tables near the window and talked for the best part of an hour. When he left, Ravezzi told Miller to phone if there was anything he could do. Miller shook the old man's hand at the door and said he would do that. He would be sure to phone, too, if there was any change in Gina. Any change at all.

7

The young Polish sailor did not die, though he came close. He'd lost a lot of blood before he reached the hospital. It was touch and go for a while. He did eventually come back to the camp but by then Frank and Josef were elsewhere and they never saw him again. Josef was kept in the guardhouse for three days and then taken before a tribunal. There were plenty of witnesses to what had happened, some of them soldiers. Although Josef had started the fight, there was no doubt that Marek had pulled a knife on him. No doubt either that Marek had gone for Josef with it and would almost certainly have killed him if he'd had the chance. Josef was released back into the camp after the tribunal. He was shaken by what had happened, appalled that he should have come so close to taking the life of another man. Frank found him uncharacteristically quiet and subdued when he came back to the house. But he thought it was probably best to let him be. Besides, Frank had his own worries then.

Ravezzi's second letter arrived soon after Josef's return to the house. Ravezzi had written the letter a few days after his visit to Paisley, having given much careful thought to what he should say and how he should say it. There was no point in upsetting Frank unnecessarily. But neither could he pretend that everything was fine.

Ultimately, he settled for an approximation of what he'd seen when he visited the café; truthful where he could be, hazy where the truth might cause Frank pain. He didn't say that Gina had run upstairs rather than meet him, just that she'd been working in the kitchen and he didn't have much opportunity to talk to her. It was a bad time to visit, he wrote; he of all people should have known better. In fact, he didn't say much about Gina in the letter. He wrote more about the changes in the café and about how well Miller was running the place. He was clearly impressed by Miller which, as far as Frank could remember, he never had been previously. The old man had neither liked nor trusted Miller but now his view was quite different.

Frank skimmed the letter as he was standing outside the guard room. Then he brought it back to the bedroom and sat on his bed, scrutinising it, trying to wring meaning from it. He couldn't decide what to make of the letter at first. On the surface, it seemed generally good. Gina was working, the café was busy, Miller was still around to help her. But there was something hesitant in what the old man wrote, something missing. Ravezzi didn't say much about Gina; he certainly didn't answer any of the questions Frank had asked. From what the old man wrote, it seemed as if he hadn't actually spoken to her. And there was no explanation for why she hadn't written recently. After he'd spent some time looking at the letter and puzzling over what it might really mean, he was more concerned than ever.

It didn't help that it had been raining and stormy for days in a row now. Most of the men had stayed inside; sometimes in bed, sometimes padding around their rooms as if they were in cages.

Frank compulsively turned over each sentence of the letter in his mind as if he were turning over pebbles in his fingers. He became obsessed with the notion that Ravezzi was holding back, not trusting him with the truth. He was angry at the old man, furious with himself for thinking that he had ever trusted him, that he had ever trusted anyone. Gina was in trouble, that much was certain. Why else wouldn't she have written to him for over two months now? Frank hated the old man for tormenting him. Ravezzi must have known what he was doing to Frank. Why would he take such pleasure in hurting him?

In this frame of mind, it seemed quite logical to Frank that he should ask Josef if he could help him slip out of the camp.

'Why?'

'I want to find a telephone box.'

The boy looked at him for a moment.

'Do you know where there is one?' Frank asked.

'You know the church steeple?'

Frank nodded. You could see this, further up the hill, from the back of the house.

'There's one beside the church.'

'I want to phone-a my wife.'

Josef wasn't keen, especially after the incident with Marek. But Frank kept on at him until he eventually agreed.

Frank and Josef slipped out the back door just after ten. They made their way to the last house in the terrace, the one furthest from the soldier's office. Josef eased into a narrow space between two wash-houses. The double row of barbed wire fencing came right up against the back of the wash-houses. There were two soldiers standing near the guard hut with a perfect view along the back of the houses.

'What about the guards?'

There were two of them standing near the guard hut at the back of the terrace of houses.

'They'll go inside the hut eventually. We just have to wait.'

It was twenty minutes before someone inside the hut called on the soldiers.

'I'll go first,' said Josef and moved quickly to the fence. He lay on his back and lifted up the wire a little and wriggled underneath the first fence. He did the same when he came to the second. When he had reached the safety of some bushes outside the compound, he signalled to Frank. Frank could hear the soldiers talking and laughing in the guard hut; they would stay in there for a while. He lay on his back and eased up the fence. Soon he was crouching beside Josef in the shadow of the bushes. Josef led him carefully between the houses and then moved out onto the pavement, walking in full view of anyone who happened to be passing.

'Are you sure this is safe?' Frank asked.

'It's safer than creeping around. Just walk normally.'

They walked up the hill, moving away from the front. The houses here weren't boarding houses or hotels. They were ordinary little detached and semi-detached cottages. They were just a few streets up from the promenade and yet it was almost as if they were in the country. They came to a small green with a duck pond, beyond which stood the church. They hadn't seen anyone else but a few cars had passed and the lights were still discreetly on in the pub across the green. On the right hand side of the church, Frank saw the phone box and began to run.

'Don't run,' Josef said. 'Take it easy.'

Frank opened the door of the phone box and stepped inside.

Josef stayed outside, in the shadows. Frank lifted up the receiver and laid out his coins. He waited for an operator to come on the line and, when she did, asked for long distance and gave her the number of the café. She told him she'd do her best but she'd need to go through three or maybe more exchanges. There was no guarantee they'd have lines. The army was using everything these days. They'd just need to wait and see how she did. Frank urged her to try anyway. It was important, he said, really important.

'Someone special?' she asked.

'My wife,' said Frank. 'And I really need to speak to her.'

'I'll see what I can do, but no promises. Put the phone down and I'll call you back when I've made the connections all the way through. If I make them . . .'

Frank slipped out of the phone box and crouched down in the bushes with Josef, who was keen to go back. Frank told him to go. He would manage on his own.

'No,' said Josef, 'I'll stay.'

Twenty minutes passed and still there was nothing. After thirty, Frank was beginning to think that they should leave and try another night. Just then, he heard the muffled sound of the phone ringing from inside the box. He rushed over and snatched the receiver.

'Still there, caller?' she asked.

'Still here,' said Frank. 'Any luck?'

'I think so.'

Frank looked outside. He heard voices as a couple of men came out of the pub. In the darkness beside him, he saw Josef drop to the ground, watching them anxiously.

'Connecting you now, caller.'

After an angry burst of static, the line cleared and he heard the phone ringing. He could picture it, sitting on its shelf just inside the kitchen, so that you could step in and use it while you kept an eye on the café. It rang out with its own distinctive burr and it was as if, for that brief moment, Frank was suddenly back there. As if all of this had just been a trick of the mind. An illusion.

✶

Gina was in bed but wasn't asleep. A wrong number, she thought at first. Who would ring at this time?

As the phone kept ringing, she rose and pulled on her dressing gown. She made her way downstairs in the dark and opened the door that led into the kitchen. She had allowed herself to think that maybe, just maybe, it could be Frank. Maybe he'd been released. Maybe he was on his way home and this was his first opportunity to call. Of course, it was far more likely to be a wrong number. Why would Frank call so late? That was just wishful thinking.

She hurried across the kitchen, the stone floor cold under her feet. The phone was on a little shelf, which Frank had made, just inside the door. She picked up the phone.

'Long distance,' said the operator. 'But I've just lost one of my lines. Give me a moment while I see if another comes free.'

Long distance?

Gina waited, listening to the hum and clicks on the other end of the phone. She was trying not to let herself hope.

✶

The men coming out of the pub were soldiers. One of them was Burke, the sergeant. Frank kept the phone to his ear, waiting to be put through. Josef had already edged back into the churchyard and was crouching behind a gravestone.

The soldiers were talking loudly, all slightly drunk. Burke noticed the man in the phone box. There was something about him, almost as if he recognised him. But this was someone in civvies, not a soldier. Frank turned his face away and looked down, though he was careful to keep his eyes on Burke. The soldiers, five of them, crossed the green. One of them threw something into the pond and shouted as he did so. If they would just keep walking, Frank said to himself. Just keep walking.

Suddenly, as he thought he was safe, Burke turned away from the others and stopped, looking right at him, hands on his hips.

'Hey, you!' he shouted. 'You in the phone box.'

Frank prayed for the connection to go through, willing Gina to answer so that he could at least hear her voice.

'Do you hear me?'

Now Burke was walking towards him. The other soldiers had stopped, not quite sure what was happening, but beginning to follow him.

'Frank, run!' he heard the boy shout.

Burke was moving faster now, able to see him. He'd recognised Frank.

Frank let the phone drop and pushed open the door. He jumped over the wall and ran through the graveyard, following Josef. The soldiers were shouting and crashing along behind them. A couple of them fell. They were drunk and couldn't see where they were going in the darkness. Josef guided Frank carefully, telling him to turn this way or that way. Soon they were in open country and everything had gone quiet behind them.

★

Gina waited in the café, still holding the phone. The operator came back on and said, 'Sorry for this. There seems to be some problem. If you could just give us a minute, we'll try to make the connection. Let me just try again.'

She sounded pleasant and quietly exasperated. Gina was happy to wait because there was still the possibility that it was Frank. Until the wrong person came on the line, it could be Frank.

After a moment, the operator said, 'I'm sorry, ma'am. Call's been disconnected at the other end.'

'That's okay,' said Gina. 'Thanks.'

'Maybe he'll call back.'

Gina said 'Yes,' and put the phone down. He, the operator had said, he. It did no harm to let herself believe that it might have been Frank. And if it had been, well, then he would call back. Frank would definitely call back.

★

The police caught up with them in the late morning. They'd headed north, over towards Ramsey where Frank thought they might have a chance of slipping onto a boat. Josef had considered giving himself up but then thought – in for a penny, in for a pound. And what difference would it make anyway if they were caught? They were already in a kind of prison.

They hid in the gardens of a large hotel that was closed and shuttered. The hotel overlooked Ramsey and they could see a good number of fishing boats in the tiny harbour. They sheltered in the warmth of a greenhouse for an hour or so but then saw soldiers around the hotel. They weren't sure if the soldiers were searching for them or were there for some other reason but they couldn't take the chance. They moved on from the greenhouse, down to a wrought iron fence that looked onto the beach and the sea. They could see the harbour to their right, a boat just easing out from the breakwater and beginning to surge up and down as it caught the swell of the open sea. The rain was heavier now, sweeping across the beach.

'Let's wait here till night,' Frank said. 'Then we'll head along to the harbour, try not to get seen.'

He had hardly spoken when the soldiers came into sight above them. Now they could see that there were two policemen with the soldiers and they had dogs. Frank and Josef tried to edge down, get behind the bushes. But one of the soldiers had seen them and was pointing at them. Suddenly, the soldiers and the police were pouring down the hill towards them. They scrambled over the fence and landed on the other side. The boy started running with Frank across the road above the beach but soon gave up. The soldiers and police were just behind him. He stood there in the middle of the shiny wet road, waiting for them to reach him.

Frank kept running. He said later that he had no idea what he was doing, didn't know where he was going or how he was ever going to escape from them. It was crazy what he tried to do. But that didn't stop him.

He jumped from the road down onto the sand, rolled over and kept running. A couple of the soldiers had stopped beside the boy. The rest came after Frank, running down steps onto the sand. But already they weren't running so fast, seeing no need to do so. There was, they saw already, nowhere for Frank to go. He ran down the beach towards the sea, zigzagging between the coils of barbed wire. His jacket caught on one of these and the coil came rolling after him, interlocking with another. As Frank tried to carry on towards the sea, the wire wrapped itself around him.

✷

It was soon after the phone call that Gina discovered she was pregnant. When she realised this, she lost her already tenuous hold on reality. She didn't go downstairs to the café any more after that.

Miller left her for a couple of days but he was aware of the women talking, heard them whispering among themselves and glancing at him. He knew they were wondering what had happened. There was something not quite right here, though they could of course only speculate on what that might be. This was exactly what Miller didn't want. In a town like Paisley this was the kind of situation where all sorts of stories could start up and be taken for gospel. That could ruin everything. And he wasn't about to let that happen.

After the third day, he closed the café early. When the place was quiet and the front door locked, he went up to see her. He knocked on the door and, when she didn't answer, used his key to let himself in. Gina looked terrible, even he had to admit that; her face was white, her eyes black and sunken. He was shocked at the change in her. It was as if all the life or spirit had been drained out of her. She had no sense of where she was. She was wearing the same clothes she'd been wearing the last time he saw her.

She started shaking as he came near her. He wasn't going to touch her, he said, trying to keep his voice down. He just wanted to know what was wrong. She pulled away from him.

'It's all right,' he kept saying. 'Just tell me what's wrong.'

But she wouldn't say anything, at least not anything that he could understand. When she spoke, she spoke in Italian as if she'd forgotten all of her English. She looks crazy, he thought. But he was getting angry with her, frustrated and angry, and fearful of the damage she could do him.

'Tell me what's wrong,' he shouted at her. 'That's all I want to know. Tell me.'

He grabbed at her but she pulled away from him. He tried to catch her as she slipped past him towards the door but couldn't turn quickly enough because of his bad leg. She just caught him ever so slightly off balance, enough to give herself the advantage. Of course, she wasn't deliberately trying to do any of this but that's not how he saw it.

She was out in the hall now, crying, heading for the door that led downstairs, desperate to get away from him. He'd left the door open. She pushed at it, just as he came up behind her. He reached out and fastened his fingers into the sleeve of her cardigan. And then Miller didn't quite know what happened. But the cardigan came away in his hand and the door swung open and she fell into the darkness, crashing down the stairs.

When he switched on the light, he could see her rag-doll body jammed in a ridiculous, impossible position up against the door that led into the café. She wasn't moving.

8

Instead of being returned to the camp, they were taken to jail in Douglas. For the first few weeks of their time there, Frank was, in his own words, 'just plain crazy'. He wouldn't cooperate with the warders or even acknowledge their presence. He was in solitary confinement and the light was kept on in his cell twenty-four hours a day.

A few days after they were recaptured, he and Josef were taken before a makeshift military tribunal in the governor's office. At this, they were both sentenced to remain in the prison 'at His Majesty's pleasure'. It was typical of the muddle and confusion of internment that the authorities had no idea what to do with Frank and Josef and never subsequently laid any specific charges against them. During the tribunal, Frank refused to answer any of the major's questions. The major himself was fairly patient and even understanding with Frank. But when he and Josef were dismissed the squaddies escorting Frank set about him in his cell – 'for his cheek', they said. Josef could hear all of this and could see the prison warders waiting in the corridor, impassive, for the soldiers to finish. But Josef, of course, could do nothing to stop it.

After the first month or so, Frank gradually became quieter and more cooperative; more like himself, as he later said. He ate everything that he was given to eat, hungry now in a way that he hadn't been before. He realised now that if he wanted to help Gina he needed to look after himself. Wasted and weak, he would be no good to her, nor to anyone else. Eventually, he was moved into Josef's cell. He was also allowed to write one letter every two weeks. Naturally he wrote to Gina at every opportunity but there never were any letters from her, nor from anyone else either. He waited at the window where the post was handed out every day. And when there was nothing for him, he would say to the warder in charge, 'Do you think there might be a letter at the camp? Could you check for me, please?'

The warder would shake his head and say, 'If there was a letter for you, it would be here. They'd send it on.'

At the end of April, Frank finally did receive a letter from Ravezzi. The letter was short and carefully worded. It told Frank that Gina had had a serious accident, falling down the stairs from the flat. She was in hospital and would be there for some time. She was doing as well as could be expected. And he would write again when there was more news. That was all it said.

Josef was worried about the effect this letter would have on Frank. But, all considered, Frank took it surprisingly well.

'It's almost a kind of relief,' Frank said. 'I knew something was wrong. Now I know what it is.'

But it was clear to both of them that the letter raised more questions than it answered.

★

He didn't try to move her from where she was lying. He could tell when he reached the bottom of the stairs that she was still alive. He eased the door open, pulling it against her body just enough to allow him to step through into the kitchen. Then he closed it again, her body helping the door to ease back into place, so that everyone would assume he had been in the kitchen or elsewhere in the café when she fell. There would be no reason for anyone to imagine that he had been with her.

He took a moment to gather his thoughts, working out his best way to face the world, thinking through the right, slightly dazed, uncertain attitude to what seemed to have happened. Mimicking, in other words, exactly how he would have felt if it had been an accident. When he was ready, he called the ambulance and ran to the pub on the corner of Causeyside Street. He told them that he'd heard a clatter from the stairs but he couldn't get the door open. Gina was lying right up against it and he was afraid he'd hurt her if he pushed it any further.

One of the barmaids and a couple of the customers tried to ease the door open but no one was keen to push too hard or to move Gina until the ambulance arrived. Miller said that he'd been taking bottles out into the yard when he heard the noise from upstairs. He didn't know what had happened, maybe she just missed her footing. But she had been acting real strange recently. You only had to ask the people in the café, he said. They hadn't seen her for days. She just refused to come downstairs and Miller hadn't wanted to force her, knowing that she was missing Frank something awful. Miller did all of this very well, not laying it on with a trowel, being almost reluctant about imparting this information, as if he was betraying a confidence in saying so much.

When the ambulance arrived, the ambulance men carefully pushed the door open until one of them could slip through. He moved Gina away from the door and then they laid her on the stretcher. Some of those who saw her were certain that she was already dead or would die soon. Her eyes were closed, didn't even flicker. She didn't speak or moan, didn't make any sound at all. As they drove her away in the ambulance, people were shaking their heads, thinking they'd seen the last of Gina Jaconelli and commiserating with Miller.

'What a terrible thing to happen,' they would say. 'Must have given you a right turn, you just working away there.'

And it was pretty much then that the talk about Gina started rippling out. The women from the pub and the shops nearby had already heard about Gina's behaviour. So Miller didn't have to say very much. In fact, he could at times seem to defend her and say that she hadn't been acting that strangely. The gossip knitted naturally and conveniently together for Miller. And there was never the least suspicion or doubt about what had actually happened here.

Gina was taken to the Royal Alexandra, a sprawling red sandstone building five minutes up the road from the café. Miller was anxious about what she might say and went up there early the next day. Initially, the doctor was reluctant to talk to him as he wasn't related to her. However when Miller explained about Frank and the fact that there was no one else close to her in the country, the doctor changed his mind. He had some questions that needed answering, he said, and Miller might be the only person who could do this. Gina had broken her spine, he said. And it was quite possible that they might still lose her. She had other superficial injuries but nothing serious. Mentally, she was clearly traumatised. She could speak but seemed not to remember anything about the accident. Or, if she did, she couldn't bring herself to talk about it.

'That's quite common in circumstances like this,' the doctor said, looking at Miller. Miller wondered if the doctor somehow suspected that Gina's fall hadn't been an accident. But, even if he did, he couldn't prove anything. Not as long as she kept quiet.

'I dare say,' said Miller noncommittally, trying to keep his voice as neutral as possible.

'There's one other thing, too,' the doctor said after a moment or two. 'It's very delicate and I'm not entirely sure that it's right to tell you. However, I don't see that I have any choice.'

'What is it?' Miller said. 'What's wrong?'

'She's pregnant.'

Again, the doctor was studying him, trying to read him like a book. Miller shook his head, astonished and shocked. Now he understood why she had suddenly retreated into herself and had behaved so irrationally.

'Her husband's interned, you say?' said the doctor.

'Since early last summer,' Miller answered.

'She's only a couple of months gone.'

The doctor waited, untroubled by the silence.

'There was an Italian, a friend of her husband's, who used to visit her. He has a café up in Glasgow,' Miller lied. 'But he hasn't been around for the last month or so.'

The doctor turned the barrel of his black fountain pen round and round between his thumb and forefingers, allowing the silence to draw itself out.

'Is the baby – a' right?' he asked.

'So far.'

The doctor was still watching him.

'What'll I tell her husband?'

'Aye, indeed, quite so,' said the doctor. 'Fortunately, that's no' my problem.'

He unscrewed the top of the fountain pen and quickly scrawled some notes on Gina's file.

'It would be better if this could be kept quiet,' Miller said.

'We've no intention of doing otherwise,' the doctor said. Miller could tell that he was unconvinced about at least part of what Miller had told him. But that didn't matter. He couldn't prove anything.

Over the next few weeks, Miller kept in close contact with the hospital. He avoided speaking to the doctor if at all possible and cultivated one or two of the nurses. From them he learned that Gina's condition continued to improve slowly and gradually. And that she never spoke about the accident, even when the nurses or doctors asked her about it. As the weeks passed, it became clear that this wasn't only related to trauma; there had been, it seemed, some brain damage, though they couldn't yet be sure of the extent of this. Over that same period, Miller started to make slight indirect references to the waitresses about the Italian – someone Frank knew – who had come to visit Gina for a while. He wouldn't say very much about him or why he came to visit. But soon this character had taken on a shadowy life of his own and the women who worked in the café regarded it as an accepted fact that Gina had been seeing someone. It could have been entirely innocent, of course, the women would quietly agree among themselves. But who knows? Long time to be on your own, they would say. Long time.

★

In June, Frank and the boy were released from prison and sent to another camp at Onchan. There was a letter waiting for Frank at the guard hut.

'It's been here a couple of weeks but I thought I'd hang onto it,' the soldier said. 'I heard you'd be coming here sometime soon.'

Frank grabbed the letter. It wasn't from Gina, he could tell that from the handwriting. In fact he didn't recognise the handwriting at all. There was something formal, official about this letter. It wasn't, he was pretty sure, from someone he knew and he opened it with apprehension.

It was from a priest, a Father Connelly. He wasn't their priest, the one from their chapel, and Frank had never heard of him before. He explained to Frank that he was a doctor as well as a priest and he worked at Moredun Convent. Frank knew this place; it was a convent and nursing home to the south of the town. You couldn't actually see it from the road but you could catch glimpses of its grey towers between the trees. Father Connelly wrote that they'd taken Gina from the main hospital and were looking after her at Moredun. He didn't say exactly what was wrong with her but he suggested that she would be better looked after in the convent. It was a more suitable place for her care and convalescence. He told Frank that she had lost the use of her legs in the accident earlier in the year. She could no longer walk and now used a wheelchair to get around. She did have a number of other problems, he wrote, and had never really recovered from the trauma of the accident. That may change in time, he said, though it was always very difficult to be sure in situations like this. He assured Frank that she was getting the very best of care and he would write again soon.

'You okay?' Josef asked, when he had finished reading the letter. They were still standing, in the sun, outside the guard hut.

'Fine.'

'Bad news?'

'Aye.'

'Your wife?'

Frank nodded. Josef put his arm round Frank's shoulder and said,

'Come on, let's get back to the house.'

✶

By the summer of 1941, Miller had moved into the flat upstairs. He put Frank and Gina's things into storage, or so he said; in fact, most of it was either sold or thrown away. He only kept the essentials, anything that was particularly personal or that he thought they might especially want, though in truth, as the sorting out went on, he wasn't overly fussy about this. He refurnished and redecorated the flat, even though Frank had done this just a couple of years before. It was almost as if this was necessary to Miller, an essential part of the process of taking over what was rightly Frank's.

The flat had always looked very different to most other homes in Paisley. When you went through the doorway, people said, it was like stepping into a foreign country. There was nothing self-conscious or deliberate about this; Frank and Gina just made the place look like the kind of homes they'd known back in Italy, as far as they could anyway. The furniture was dark and heavy. The wallpaper was embossed and richly patterned. The curtains were thick velvet drapes, some of them edged with lace, and tied back with broad, shiny pieces of ribbon in a style that most local people would have regarded as 'fancy' or 'ower-showy for us'. There were pictures on most of the walls, nearly all of Italy and particularly of Pozzuoli and the Bay of Naples. There were good Turkish carpets on the floors and dark green palms and castor oil plants in pots and on stands here and there around the rooms.

By the time Miller had finished, all of this had gone. The wallpaper was a tiny, pale floral pattern, indistinct and recessive. The furniture was lighter, plainer. There were no pictures on the walls, none at all, and the floors had been laid with light brown linoleum and plain carpets. Everything was neutral, bland, characterless. The flat had been transformed but then that, surely, was the point.

Downstairs, in the café, it was much the same. By the end of that summer, there was hardly anything that remained unchanged. There was no longer any vestige of Frank or Gina in the café. And it bore little resemblance to how it had looked when it had been The Bay of Naples. All of this, naturally, prompted people to ask questions. But Miller handled this well, mostly saying very little. He kept his story simple and refused to go into details; somehow to do so would have been an admission that his version of events needed bolstering. All that anyone needed to know, he said, was that he had bought the café from Gina, paid a fair price for it. That's all there was to it. He wouldn't say whether this had happened before or after the accident, or whether Frank had known about it. That was private, he said, between him and Gina and Frank. The papers were all with his solicitor and everything was completely in order.

Most people soon forgot about Gina. She'd never had any close friends among the Italians in the town. Her only visitors were old man Ravezzi and, occasionally, Robert Glen. Ravezzi went every Wednesday afternoon and spent a couple of hours with her. Sometimes he would talk to her, hold her hand and just say anything that came into his head. Other times, he would sit there in silence. It didn't matter which he did; she never responded to him, never really gave any indication that she knew he was there. He had his own suspicions about what had happened but they were no more than suspicions. He couldn't prove, or do, anything.

He had gone to Miller's solicitor one day, when he heard about Miller having 'bought' the café, and he asked to see the contract. The solicitor said that he was under no obligation to show him anything. However, as a token of good faith, he would allow Ravezzi to have sight of the contract for the purchase of the café. It did appear to have been signed by Gina and was, as far as he could make out, in order and properly countersigned. But the solicitor wouldn't let him see the full document.

'How much did he pay for the business?' Ravezzi asked.

'That's confidential.'

'Where's the money? I cannae find any trace of it.'

'That's nothin' to do wi' us,' the solicitor said, looking him straight in the eye. 'I suggest ye ask the lady.'

Robert Glen had also looked into this but with no more success. One night, when his anger and frustration got the better of him, he went to see Miller and asked him about the contract and Gina. Miller calmly repeated the same story that he had told everyone else. Robert listened to this for a time and then, suddenly, with no warning, grabbed Miller by the throat and banged him up against the wall. Miller was frightened but kept his nerve.

'What you goin' to do now, eh?' Miller said, smiling.

'Whatever I do, there'll be no one to see it.'

'Then it'll be your word against mine,' said Miller. 'An' I'll make sure the whole story comes out. People'll hear all about her up there in Moredun.'

Robert released him, knowing that he could do nothing here other than make the situation even worse. Miller said quite calmly, 'This is my property and I want you out a here.'

This was more than Robert Glen could bear.

'If ye don't go, I'll phone the police.'

To underline his point, Miller picked up the phone. After another few moments, he started to dial.

Robert turned and walked out, leaving Miller in full and undisputed possession of the café.

9

When he was released from internment in January 1942, a year and a half after he'd first been arrested, Frank already knew pretty much what had happened with the café.

Old man Ravezzi had written and, as gently as he could, explained that Miller had 'taken over' the business. He was no longer merely minding it for Frank. Ravezzi still didn't understand how Miller had managed this and he made his feelings about Miller quite clear. He was sorry to have to tell Frank all of this, he had written, but it was surely better that Frank knew. Maybe he could do something when he came back. But Ravezzi wasn't hopeful. Miller had all the relevant papers and contracts and they appeared to be in order. Both he and Robert Glen had looked into this. Robert Glen had even asked someone from CID to talk to Miller and his solicitor but they weren't in the least rattled by the detective. They had Gina's signature on the contract. And, if no one could find what Gina had done with the money, well, that wasn't their responsibility. Nor their problem.

The café wasn't Frank's concern. The café was nothing. It was a room with some tables and chairs and pictures on the wall. Things, objects.

But Gina . . . Gina was a different matter entirely. What could have happened to her? How could she be so changed that she hadn't written for months? Not a word. And there was still nothing very specific in the letters from Ravezzi, or in those from Father Connelly in the convalescent home. And why did she need to be there, in what was effectively a hospital? Father Connelly had written several letters to Frank. But these letters were short and gave him no real information other than that Gina 'was coming along fine' or 'seemed more settled'.

No, the café didn't matter a damn. That was gone, history. But what would he find when he saw Gina again? That was the question that lay like a stone on his heart during his last few months in Onchan.

✷

Frank and Josef were initially told they'd be released early in January 1942. This was then changed to 'late February or maybe early March'. Finally, on the evening of the 24th of January, a soldier opened the front door and shouted that anyone still left in this house would be released the following morning.

At seven thirty, Frank and Josef joined the detachment of men loitering around the gates. There was no forming ranks now, no being shouted at, no need to keep quiet. They'd watched other detachments march out of the gates most days for the last month or so. But neither of them could quite believe they were about to be freed. Someone would change their mind at the last minute. Their names wouldn't be on the list. Or they would be wrongly spelled. Or there would be some other capricious, absurd reason that would condemn them to remain while the others left. Perhaps they would simply be kept here forever.

In the event, the gates soon swung open and, with one soldier accompanying them, they made their way down the hill and along the promenade to the harbour. Frank mostly avoided looking at the beach because it reminded him of his pathetic, hopeless attempt at escape. He had never in his life felt so impotent as he had done that morning; never experienced before such an acute sense of counting for so little in the scheme of things. He could tell himself that it was all in the past. And it was better left there. But the memory of his helplessness as he lay on the wet sand, caught in the wire, under the bright, indifferent sky stayed with him like a deep scar that would never entirely heal.

The crossing to Liverpool was rough but Frank and Josef stayed on the top deck, in the shelter of the funnel, watching the Isle of Man disappear into the sea behind them. Even when there was nothing to look at but the seagulls and the white foaming wake of the boat on an expanse of rolling grey sea, they remained where they were, impervious to the cold and the spray that soaked them through. They said very little to each other, their thoughts mostly on the future. Now that they had been released, the next few days and weeks suddenly became a more difficult proposition. They were like prisoners suddenly set free from jail and forced to confront a world that was no longer rigorously confined and structured.

All of the internees shared, to a greater or lesser degree, these feelings of apprehension. They had been snatched away from their lives and they were now, just as randomly and with no say in the matter, being pitched back into those same lives. Except, of course, those lives weren't the same. They couldn't be, not after all this time, not during a war. So what, they wondered, would they find? What would have changed? How could they be sure that they would pick up the pieces again and carry on as before? The contemplation of these questions, and many more, kept all of the internees subdued and quiet throughout the journey.

When they disembarked in Liverpool, there were no soldiers waiting for them. They walked unsupervised down the swaying wooden gangplank. When their feet hit the dockside, they were free to do as they liked and go where they wanted. The docks were busy with ships and lorries and men. No one looked twice at them. Like many internees, Josef had already signed up to join the British army on his release. There were a couple of open-topped lorries waiting for the new recruits and these were soon filled. The sight of sixty or so men, suddenly transformed from interned aliens into British soldiers, merely underlined the absurdity of the whole business.

Josef elbowed his way into the back of one of the lorries, starting an argument with someone who thought there were already enough people in that particular lorry. He shouted down that he would write, care of Robert Glen as Frank had said. Frank told him to watch out for himself. After a moment or so, the lorry abruptly drove off while Josef and the other internee were still going at it. Josef's command of both English and the demotic were pretty impressive, Frank remembered thinking. And then the lorry and Josef were lost from sight in the busy docks.

Josef stayed in the army for the rest of the war. He was wounded in Italy but eventually went home to Austria in the summer of 1945. He did write to Frank a couple of times after the war and Frank replied to each letter. But Frank's last letter was returned, stamped 'Not known at this address' in German, and Frank never heard from him again.

Frank arrived back in Paisley late the following afternoon. It was raining and the light was already going as he stepped out of the station and into County Square. Little had changed apart from the obvious; there was criss-cross tape on the windows of the post office, more people were in uniform and the streetlights were off. Otherwise, it was all surprisingly normal. People were going in and out of shops, stopping for a blether if they saw a familiar face. They were waiting for buses and trams and fighting their way on when one arrived. No one bothered Frank. No one even looked twice at him. He glanced across at the police station, on the far side of County Square. And he wondered, for a moment, about seeing if Robert Glen was on duty. But that could wait, he thought. There was only one place he wanted to go right now, only one place he could go.

✶

Frank rang the bell on the pillar beside the wrought-iron gates. It was still raining. There were no lights on the road or in any of the few houses that he'd passed on his way up here. These houses were substantial Victorian and Edwardian mansions, set back from the road in extensive wooded grounds. You couldn't actually see many of the houses from the road, just their entrance gates, most of which were equally imposing and unwelcoming.

A serious-looking young man, one of the gardeners Frank later learned, came out of the gatehouse and asked his business.

'My wife is here. Gina Jaconelli,' he said. 'I'd like to see her.'

'Wait here,' the young man said and went back into the gatehouse. Frank sheltered from the rain under one of the trees, watching the occasional car sweep by, lights off, tyres hissing on the wet road. After ten minutes or so, the young man come back and opened one of the gates just enough to allow Frank through.

'Follow the path up.'

'Where am I goin'?'

'Someone'll meet you.'

The path was laid deeply with red sandstone chips which crunched and gave underfoot and made walking slightly difficult. The ground rose to a ridge from where Frank could see the slightly forbidding mock-Gothic convent and its newer outbuildings. As he followed the slope of the path down, Frank saw a heavy figure hurrying towards him. The man, well over six foot, was carrying an umbrella tilted in front of him so that it obscured his face. He was moving quickly and deliberately and Frank fully expected him to keep going and walk right past him. He was surprised when the man stopped, put out his hand and said, 'Father Connelly. Pleased to meet you.'

A Highlander.

'You wrote they letters to me,' Frank said, shaking his hand.

'I did. I'm sorry if I kept you waiting. I was with a patient,' he said, already turning and heading back the way he'd come. 'Come on. Let's away up the house and out of this rain.'

He held the umbrella over Frank so that it sheltered both of them and led him towards a side door of the house. The priest asked about his journey from Liverpool and chatted about the general difficulties of making any journey now as if they had known each other for years and were just lightly passing the time of day. They went along a corridor, up stairs and along more corridors until they came to an office with books lining the walls and a fire spitting and crackling in the grate.

'Take your coat off and warm yourself up,' the priest said, waving him over to the fire.

'Where's Gina?'

The priest looked at him for a moment.

'All in good time, my friend. All in good time.'

The priest busied himself for a couple of minutes sorting through the papers on his desk. Frank was initially irritated by this. But he soon saw that he was simply being given time to collect his thoughts and make himself comfortable, as far as he could anyway with his clothes soaked through. Much later, Frank came to appreciate how lucky they had been to fall into the hands of Father Connelly. If Gina had come under the care of someone less good-hearted, 'more like most priests' as Frank would sometimes say, things could easily have gone much worse for them.

'You know that Gina is very ill, Frank?'

Frank nodded.

'I tried to make that clear in my letters.'

'You never told me what's wrong with her. I know it's bad.'

'Aye, quite so,' the priest said, finally sitting down opposite him.

'So what is it? What's happened?'

'It's not just the one thing. I can't just say to you it's this or that. It's more complicated than that . . .'

Frank listened to everything the priest told him. On one level, he was taking it in, slowly laying each painful piece of the jigsaw in its place. But, on another, he felt as if he was merely dreaming. Everything around him was both real and unreal, colours and sensations somehow more vivid and heightened. And he felt that same inability to move, that sense of paralysis, that he usually only experienced in dreams.

Father Connelly couldn't say what had caused Gina to fall down the stairs from the flat to the café. The police had looked into this thoroughly but failed to come up with any very satisfactory explanation. Miller said he hadn't seen anything, had simply heard the noise of her falling and found her behind the door. The fact was, however the accident had happened, Gina had broken her spine in the fall. She couldn't walk and it was unlikely she'd ever do so again. There had been other damage too, he added quietly.

'Gina's abilities . . . her mental abilities . . . are greatly diminished. She can't speak, nothing that you would really understand, anyway. And she appears not to recognise anyone. She almost certainly won't recognise you and you should prepare yourself for that. There's a chance she might improve in the future but it's slender and the more time goes on, well . . .'

He held his hands out in an unmistakable gesture of hopelessness.

'I should also warn you that Gina now has fits on a fairly regular basis.'

Frank shook his head.

'On average, she has one of these "grand mal" seizures every couple of days. She can go a week or more without one but then she'll have other days when she might have a run of them. The fits can be distressing the first few times you see them but you'll get used to them.'

Frank would often say that was the one thing Father Connelly got wrong. He never got used to the fits. Never. Didn't see how anyone could.

Frank was sitting in a green leather armchair that seemed to cradle him like a giant's hand. His body was utterly limp.

He was sure that if he tried to stand up he would collapse on the floor. The priest continued talking, his quiet steady voice punctuated by the hissing and spitting of the fire. Frank could feel its piercing heat on the side of his face and he felt dizzy and slightly queasy.

'There is, too, something else you should know,' the priest said, keeping his eyes on Frank.

'What?' said Frank after a moment, not believing that there could be anything more or that he hadn't yet heard the worst of it.

'When Gina came to us, there was another problem.'

Later, Frank said that he already knew what the priest was going to say. He had never considered the possibility until that moment. But, even as the priest spoke, he knew.

'She was pregnant.'

'No,' Frank said. It wasn't really a denial, more a cry of pain.

'I'm afraid so.'

There wasn't the slightest trace of doubt in the priest's eyes. There was simply no escaping the fact, no turning away from it.

'How?'

'I can't answer that question, Frank. And Gina, of course, can tell us nothing.'

And Gina, of course, can tell us nothing. With those words, Frank finally began to grasp the scale of the change he would find in Gina. His immediate reaction was to blame himself for having brought her to this country. It was his fault, nobody's fault but his. He should never have written to the priest in Pozzuoli. He should never have pursued her, kept writing when she had clearly changed her mind. He should never have asked her to come to Scotland. It had all been a mistake, his mistake. 'Look how it's ended,' he said to himself. 'Look what I've done to her.' Then he glanced up at the priest, waiting for him to continue.

'Gina was delivered of the baby a few months ago.'

Frank was dropping through space.

'As you can imagine, the pregnancy and delivery were difficult because of her other problems.'

'Something went wrong?'

'No, Gina came through fine.'

This was one of the few times the priest chose the wrong words. He quickly sensed this and corrected himself.

'Or I suppose I should say that the pregnancy caused her no further complications.'

Frank was empty, a shell. The priest waited, watching him closely.

'Shall I leave you for a few moments?'

'No,' Frank said, almost surprised by his own clarity of purpose, 'I want to see Gina.'

✲

The priest took him to an outbuilding. It was all on one-level and it had a central corridor with rooms opening off on both sides. Father Connelly walked to the end of the corridor and opened a door.

As he stood in the doorway, Frank saw a young girl in a wheelchair near the window. A nurse was brushing the girl's hair. The girl was wearing a blue towelling dressing gown over a nightdress and her feet and ankles were bare. Her legs were thin, barely skin and bone, and twisted slightly to one side of the wheelchair. Her hands were resting in her lap but her right hand was bent round on itself and lay cupped in her open left hand. Frank didn't understand why the priest had brought him here. The priest had clearly made a mistake and they'd come into the wrong room. But the priest was moving over to the girl, laying his hand gently on her shoulder, though she didn't react to this in any way, and then saying a few quiet words to the nurse. It was something in the eyes that Frank recognised first and yet her eyes were as changed as everything else. There was no life in them, no gleam of light, no sense of recognising him. But they *were* Gina's eyes. Her hair had been cut short. And Gina, he remembered, his heart breaking, had always been so proud of her long dark hair. It had all gone, emphasising the thinness and boniness of her face. This was Gina, but it was nothing like the Gina he'd left behind, nothing even like the Gina he'd seen in the hospital immediately after the miscarriage.

She held her head over to one side, almost resting on her shoulder. Her mouth hung slightly open. She hadn't looked round once since they came into the room. The nurse was standing behind her, brushing her hair, which clearly gave her pleasure; Frank would find later that having her hair brushed was something she always enjoyed and it was one of the few ways of calming her when she became agitated.

'Gina,' said the priest, 'someone's come to see you.'

Gina showed no sign of having heard. The nurse stopped brushing her hair and Gina looked up, but slightly off to one side, not directly at the nurse. It was as if something had changed in her world but she didn't know what that something was.

'Gina,' the priest said again. She looked up but she didn't, Frank was sure, really see either of them. She looked towards

192

the voice but the voice meant nothing to her. It was just a sound that had caught her attention for the moment.

'Can I touch her?'

The priest nodded. Frank laid his hand on top of hers. She showed no response whatsoever.

'It's good to see you,' he said, trying to believe his own words. And he leaned forward to kiss her forehead. Her hair smelled different, of hospitals and soap, not the trace of perfume which had always been there before.

Frank was aching to hold her. He wanted to lift her up, hold her body against his, take her weight in his arms. God knows he had always been able to do that in the past and would have no difficulty doing it now. She must weigh nothing, he thought. There was nothing of her.

'The nurse has to get Gina ready for bed now, Frank. Usually she'd have been in bed by now.'

Frank nodded, dazed, unsure what more to say or do.

'You can come back anytime you like,' said the priest.

Frank stood there for a long moment, watching her. She took no interest in him at all.

Father Connelly walked Frank part of the way along the path.

'If you want to visit her, just let me know.'

Frank nodded and shook hands with the priest.

'Where are you going now? It's late.'

'I don't know,' said Frank, though this wasn't true.

'I could find you somewhere.'

'That'll no' be necessary,' Frank said and went on down the path towards the gate. The rain had stopped and the stones sounded even noisier now beneath his feet.

The priest watched him for a few moments and then hurried back to the main building and made a phone call.

✳

The door of the café was still open and there was a light dimly shining from the kitchen. The same and not the same, it was absolutely his café, his 'Bay of Naples', and yet nothing like it. He couldn't really take in too many of the changes, couldn't register all of the ways, large and small, in which Miller had altered it. He was dazed and tired, unable to erase from his mind that last image of the broken, vacant Gina relaxing as the nurse started to brush her hair again. He didn't know why he was here or what he planned to do. But there was nowhere else he could be at this moment in time. After the convent, this was the only place he could go, the only place in the whole empty dark meaningless universe.

The kitchen door creaked open and light oozed into the café. Miller was standing in the doorway with the light behind him. He was better dressed than Frank remembered. More sure of himself, too. The changes, Frank thought, weren't just in the café.

'I've been waitin' for you,' Miller said.

Frank looked at him, puzzled.

'I heard you were back. I knew you'd come the night.'

Miller stepped through the doorway and Frank saw that there were two men sitting at the kitchen table. They had been playing cards and drinking.

'Friends,' Miller said. And it was impossible for even Frank to miss the note of menace in his voice. But Frank was beyond caring. Way beyond. One of the men came to the door behind Miller.

'Just in case,' Miller said, leaning on the counter. He was surprisingly comfortable, at his ease. This, too, was different; totally unlike the Miller Frank remembered.

Frank put his brown canvas case on the floor and moved over to the near end of the counter, by the cash till. He touched the counter, letting his hand rest on the dark, cold mahogany, remembering this was exactly how it had always felt – cool, smooth, reassuring.

'Place has changed,' Frank said finally, looking around.

'Had to,' Miller said, wary of Frank's neutral tone of voice. 'No choice, no two ways about it.'

'The mirror, too?'

Now the second man rose from the table and stood just behind Miller in the doorway. Miller didn't look round but he knew both men were there.

'Okay,' Frank could see him thinking. 'We'll take this at your pace, play it your way.'

And that, too, was not the Miller he remembered. That poise, that degree of calculation, was something he'd never seen in him before.

'You remember John Blair? Used to come in here with his wife and son?'

Of course Frank remembered him. But it was a memory from another world, another life.

'He lost his son. Killed at sea, by an Italian boat. Came in here the night he heard an' smashed that and just about everything else.'

Frank shook his head. This didn't tally with the quiet, courteous, dryly funny man he remembered. But if the man had lost a son . . . Well, Frank could see that, could understand

195

how that would get to anyone. And it was just a mirror, a thing, nothing of any consequence.

'What d'you want, Frank?'

Frank shrugged, unable to answer the question even to himself. This assurance too was quite different. This taking the lead; this shocking, almost bored confidence.

'This is my place now,' Miller continued. 'I bought it fair an' square. I have a' the papers, everything.'

Frank half-smiled and shook his head, still trying to understand the puzzle of Miller, the puzzle of how a man could re-make himself, become so completely what he had never been. Or had he always been like this and Frank simply hadn't noticed?

'I don't care about this place.'

'So what do you want?'

Frank let a moment or so pass. There was no smile on his face now.

'What did you do to Gina?'

'Bad accident, that,' he shrugged. 'Don't know what happened there. Nothin' I could do about it.'

Absolutely no remorse whatsoever. No shadow or hint.

Just behind the counter, on the other side of the cash till, there was a shallow wooden drawer above the display cabinet. There were two compartments in this drawer; the furthest compartment contained small cake knives and forks, the nearest was where they kept the long knives for cutting cakes into portions. Miller could have shifted them, of course; that, too, could have changed. Frank stepped behind the counter, still looking at the mirror.

''Mon, this is a waste a time,' one of the men said. 'Let's get him out a here. I'm ready for a drink.'

The other man nodded and switched off the light in the kitchen. All of them were moving towards Frank now. Frank pulled the drawer open. The knives gleamed snugly in their wooden compartments, exactly where they had always been.

✱

Robert Glen was at home, in bed, when Father Connelly phoned the police station. The duty sergeant called Robert and passed on the priest's message. Robert asked for a car to collect him. Then he quickly dressed.

Robert lived out by the Hurlet, a good five miles out of town, so he was ready and waiting when the car arrived. He tried to work out how long it would have taken for Frank to walk from the convent to the café and hoped that he might still reach the café before him. When they pulled up outside the café, Robert shouted at the driver to come with him.

✱

Frank cut one of the men across the back of the hand. The line of blood opened and swelled before the man pulled his hand away, shocked. The two men were between him and Miller. Frank was trying to push by them and get to Miller in the narrow space between the counter and the back wall. He didn't want to hurt the other men. He'd only struck out with the knife because the man managed to get his arm round Frank's neck and was dragging him towards the floor. He was thinking about nothing except Miller. He wanted to kill Miller. There was never really much doubt in Frank's mind, afterwards, about his intention that night.

Suddenly, someone else locked an arm round Frank's neck

and he was being dragged backwards. This was someone who meant it, who knew exactly what he was doing.

'Frank, put the knife down.'

He knew that voice.

'Drop it, Frank!' The arm round his neck was jerked even tighter so that Frank could barely breathe. Frank said later that when he realised this was Robert Glen it was as if he woke up. He let the knife go and stopped struggling.

'I want him arrested,' Miller said. 'For assault.'

'Aye, look what he did to my haun,' said the man who'd been cut.

'If you think I'm arrestin' anybody, you've another think comin'.'

'Look at this. Look at the blood.'

'I don't see a thing. How about you, constable?'

'Me neither.'

Robert Glen knew the two men. More to the point, both men knew Robert. They had crossed paths in the past and it wasn't a fond memory for either of them. Robert advanced, poking his finger hard into the shoulder of the man whose hand was bleeding.

'You say anythin' about this, I'll make your life a misery. Both of youse. An' I can do that, can't I?'

They nodded.

'Get!'

The two men slipped past him and out the door without a word. Robert turned to Miller who was about to let rip.

'No' a word.'

Miller stood face to face with Robert for a moment or two. Then he turned angrily away.

Robert and the other policeman lifted Frank up, taking his full weight. He was drained, unable to walk or support himself without help.

'Let's go,' said Robert to the other policeman. 'Help me get him into the car.'

10

Robert Glen took Frank home with him that night. He slept in the Glens' spare bedroom.

In the morning, while they were having breakfast, Robert said, 'You're welcome to stay here, Frank. Long as you like.'

Frank shook his head and smiled.

'We've got mair space than we know what to dae wi'.'

'He means it,' said Mary, Robert's wife.

'Thanks,' Frank said after a long moment.

'So it's settled?' said Mary.

'I'll stay. But only for a day or two.'

'Why?' said Robert.

'I need-a to get on,' Frank said. 'I've things to do.'

'What kind of things?' Robert asked, worried that last night might not have been the end of anything. But he had misunderstood Frank and should, as he said later, have known better.

'I need a job, somewhere to live.'

'In Paisley?'

Frank looked at him.

'Where else would I go?'

'Aye, sure,' Robert said with a smile seeing now, for the first time, something of the Frank he remembered from before. That directness and honesty, almost a kind of innocence bordering on naivety, was still there, undiminished, despite everything.

Over the next few days, Robert helped Frank find a small flat and a job. The single end – a room and scullery, toilet outside on the stairs – was on the Renfrew Road and the job was washing up in the canteen of a whisky bottling plant. Neither the flat nor the job was ideal but they would do. They were a start and that was all Frank needed. Before Robert left Frank that day, he asked about Miller.

'You worried I'm-a gonnae go back?'

'Are you?'

'I'll-a never set foot in that place again.'

'Good. Best thing.'

'But I'll find out what happened there. I-a owe it to Gina.'

Robert nodded and told Frank he would help him any way that he could. But he wasn't hopeful. Miller had covered his tracks well.

'You're probably right. But I still have to try.'

'Aye sure, so ye do,' Robert said, though he doubted anything would come of this, except maybe more heartache.

Frank settled quickly into his new life. The war continued, of course, but Frank paid it no great attention. Robert Glen had a word with someone on the Conscription Board to ensure that Frank wasn't taken away from Gina a second time. On the few occasions when the town was bombed, Frank stayed in his room and watched the factory chimneys and buildings crumple in, almost delicately, on themselves, believing that somehow he wouldn't be hurt or perhaps, inside, not caring any more. He kept himself pretty much to himself after he came back from the Isle of Man. He would see Robert from time to time and once or twice he visited old man Ravezzi in Gourock. Otherwise he concentrated on work, soaking up all the overtime he could get, spending as little as possible, saving as carefully as he'd done back in the early thirties. When he found a better-paid job on the bottling line, he jumped at it. After a few months, he moved on again, to the mill.

For the rest of the war, he went from job to job, taking anything that would allow him to earn more and save more. He stayed well away from the café. In fact, he wouldn't even walk past it and always avoided that part of town. He hired his own solicitor to look into the sale of the café but, as Robert had predicted, this led nowhere. The contract was in order and would stand up in any court. It had been signed by Gina, so it seemed, and witnessed by Pollock's secretary who swore that she had watched Gina sign it. There was some doubt over the amount of money paid for the café but something had been paid into the Clydesdale Bank at the Cross in Gina's name. It had then been transferred to another account, also in Gina's name, and after that they lost track of it. Frank's solicitor said that, chances were, the money had probably gone straight back to Pollock and Miller, but of course there was no way of knowing that for sure. In the end, the solicitor advised Frank to let it go. And, with some reluctance, Frank finally did just that.

All through this time, Frank had been visiting Gina regularly. After the first few months, she became used to having him around. But she remained wary and he would sometimes catch her watching him from the corner of her eye, slightly perplexed, even frightened. At those times, Frank wondered if it might not be kinder to leave her alone. Was he really doing this for her? Or for himself? He never succeeded in answering this question satisfactorily. But the fact was that Frank couldn't imagine his life without Gina. She was a given, part of the warp and weft of his world. As Frank saw things, it was impossible to remove Gina from that world without destroying it. If he walked away and left her in the convent, he would lose everything.

Frank never gave up hope that Gina would eventually improve or at least come round to him, even a little. The child, whom the nuns had named Theresa, was a problem for Frank. He saw Gina alone initially. But Gina liked to have Theresa beside her. When she was with Theresa she was relatively content. But when Theresa was taken away she was uneasy, distracted, slightly distressed. In the end, Frank accepted the inevitable and allowed the child to remain in the room when he visited Gina. There was no taking Gina without Theresa and so gradually he learned to take both of them. And as he would sometimes say later to close friends like Robert Glen, although it might seem strange to some people, he never had any cause to regret this.

✶

Gina remained in the wheelchair for the rest of her life. She gradually began to speak a little, though you had to work at understanding her. Frank and Theresa could make out what she was saying but most people couldn't. Despite his best efforts, and his talk of Pozzuoli and their time before he was interned, Frank was never convinced that she remembered anything of their earlier life. That was gone, locked away somewhere in the depths of her mind.

Gradually Frank, Gina and the child became a unit, pretty much like any other family. At least that was how Frank saw it.

And Theresa was part of it all, not something you could separate off from the rest. As far as Theresa was concerned, Frank was her father; she never thought otherwise and Frank never did anything to disillusion her or cause her to doubt this. He treated her exactly as if she were his daughter. People talked, of course, about Frank and what had happened to his wife while he'd been away and how he was bringing up another man's child. Gradually, some version of the story seeped out and made its way through the closes and the backyards and the bars, though of course no one ever really knew the truth or could prove anything against Miller.

Frank knew what people were saying but he ignored it. He kept on exactly as before, visiting Gina as often as he could; spending time with her, pushing her round the grounds of Moredun in a wheelchair, talking to her, playing with Theresa, watching the girl grow and change in that astonishingly quick way that children do. Sometimes, Robert Glen or old man Ravezzi would ask Frank if he was sure he was doing the right thing. Frank would always look them straight in the eye and say, 'Aye, sure,' as if he wondered at them for asking the question. Frank would never say much more than this; he wouldn't become angry or protest or try to justify himself. As he saw it, there was no great issue here, nothing to be discussed, no other possible way of dealing with the situation. Robert Glen said that it was as if Frank had decided to unpick the past and remake it. And because he set about it so single-mindedly and with such determination, he succeeded in doing exactly that. As much as anyone ever could, of course.

By the time the war ended, the gossip had pretty well stopped and people had forgotten about Frank and Gina and the girl, who was now coming up for four. In the summer of 1945, Frank was working as a barber at a shop in the west end. When people asked him what he knew about cutting hair, he would say, 'As much as I ever knew about running a café and making ice cream when I came here at first.'

By early 1946, he'd saved enough to buy a small bungalow out near the shop. When he'd decorated and furnished this, he moved Gina and Theresa into it. As you can imagine, there was some resistance from the nuns and some of the doctors but Father Connelly lent Frank his support. More to the point, he also helped Frank find a steady supply of good and reliable nurses who would look after Gina and Theresa while he was working.

It was a full-time job looking after Gina. She had to be helped with every drink she took and every piece of food she ate. She had to be washed and changed when she soiled herself. The only person she would allow to wash her hair was Frank, so this became a routine with them every couple of nights. On the whole, Frank coped with it all pretty well. And, as she grew older, Theresa was a great help too. Gina often had fits. Neither Frank nor Theresa ever became used to these fits. Each time, it was like the first time. And each time, their hearts ached that Gina had to suffer in this way. They began with a kind of gasp, like a sharp intake of breath. Frank and Theresa knew what it was from the sound alone. Her whole body shook with unimaginable violence. If she was in the wheelchair, it would be rattling. Her arms and legs would be going, everything, the works. Her face would be pale and her lips clenched together. Once the first part of the fit was over, there would be that awful hoarse breathing. And she would still be shaking but not as bad. If she was in the chair, they would keep her there. It was hopeless trying to move her while she was fitting. You could easily drop her. It just wasn't worth even trying. So they would take her hand and speak to her, just nothing, nonsense, anything that came into their heads. Just so's she would hear a voice. Sometimes they would stroke her hair over and over and say, 'There, there . . .' The doctor at Moredun had told Frank that people could hear what was being said to them during fits and it was good to reassure them and comfort them. So that's what they always did. But, no, they never got used to the fits. Never.

As the years went on, people thought of them as just another family. Sure, they had problems. But then every family has its problems. And, as always, there was the simple fact that people liked Frank. People enjoyed chatting with him. 'Always good for a laugh,' they would say. And, of course, everyone could see how hard he worked to look after his wife and daughter.

By the time Theresa was nine or ten, they had moved house several times. This was always done with the purpose of finding somewhere that would be easier for Gina: more on a level, with bigger rooms, that kind of thing. People still talked, of course, but not nearly so much. Frank's story was old news. And most people had forgotten about The Bay of Naples or the fact that Frank had ever worked anywhere other than the barber's in the west end, just on the right there, after you passed the Regal Cinema.

★

After the war, Miller built the café into, as they say, 'quite a business'. He extended it into the courtyard, adding a new kitchen and extending the floor space. He was forever doing up the café and 'improving' it. In the late forties and early fifties, it was one of the most popular and successful cafés in the town. He had a proper chef and the waitresses wore black dresses and white aprons, just like in Henderson's in Glasgow. Miller himself became quite the local figure. He was in the masons, of course, and the Rotary and Chamber of Commerce. For a couple of years, he was a town councillor and sat on several of the bigger committees. He invested some of his profits in property, which was cheap after the war and a good way of making money because so many people were desperate for somewhere to rent. In the early fifties, he married one of the waitresses. They lived in a handsome red sandstone mansion in Potterhill and Miller drove around the town in a black Rover.

In 1954, he and his wife sold up and emigrated. He'd met someone from South Africa who wanted to set up a whole chain of cafés and had told him how much money he could make out there. Miller and his wife didn't stay in South Africa for very long. Something didn't work out – no one really knew what it was – and they moved on, some people said to Rhodesia, others to Australia or even New Zealand. No one kept in touch with them and no one gave them much thought after they left.

*

In the early fifties, when the owner retired, Frank bought the barber shop where he'd been working. He took on a couple of barbers to work for him and, after a few years, he bought the next-door shop and turned that into a women's hairdressers'.

At first, he worked between the two shops. But once he had the women's side up and running, he tended to stay in the barber's shop, happy to let the girls get on with it. As Theresa grew up, she turned into a striking-looking young woman; the image of her mother, at least according to those who had known Gina before her accident. She was a tiny thing, almost like a bird, and very pretty. And she had her mother's hair, too: dark auburn. When she left school, Frank brought her to work in the hairdressers'. He had wanted her to stay on at school and maybe go to college. But Theresa knew exactly what she wanted to do and that was just to work in the shop beside her father. Which is exactly what she did. And, in fact, she did it so well that, by the time she was married and had a son of her own, she was running the salon by herself and both businesses were thriving.

And that was pretty much how things were, and seemed likely to stay, until Miller suddenly, and without any warning, came back to Paisley.

☆

In 1967, Miller was living with his second wife, a young Australian woman, in a town on the west coast of Australia about 50 miles north of Perth. They had no children.

One morning in May, Miller kissed his wife and left for work as usual. He owned a Chrysler showroom in the town and had done well with it. That morning, though, he didn't go to work. He drove through the town in his pastel blue Valiant, passing in front of the showroom. One of the salesmen saw the car going by. He assumed Miller was going to see a customer but there was nothing in the book for that morning.

Miller never went back to the showroom or to his wife. He drove into Perth and took the first of a series of flights that brought him eventually to Prestwick on the afternoon of Thursday, the 16th of May. There had been no argument with his wife. He had no money worries. As far as she was concerned, it had just been a normal morning, like hundreds of others before it.

*

That Thursday evening, Frank was on his own, washing out one of the sinks. He'd already shut the shop and was just waiting for Theresa to finish up next door. Usually, she drove Frank back home and came in to see her mother. Some nights, she and Frank would bathe Gina and that would take some time. Other nights, she would just stop for twenty minutes or so. She'd talk to her mother, make sure she was comfortable while Frank said goodbye to the nurse and started preparing his own and Gina's supper. Then Theresa would go on to her own house, which wasn't far away. Theresa was married at this time and had a boy of about nine months. He was called Franco, after his grandfather. Her husband's mother helped look after the boy while Theresa worked in the salon.

Frank noticed the man standing across the road, waiting to cross, he thought. But even in that first glance, he must have registered something, something that caught in his mind. He turned on the tap to flush out the sink and looked again. The man was still standing there. If he'd wanted to cross, he could have done so by now. But he was still in exactly the same position, with no apparent intention of moving. It seemed as if he was looking at the shop, perhaps even at him, though Frank couldn't be sure about that. Buses and cars passed, briefly obscuring him. Still he was standing there. And then, as Frank watched the water swirl down the plughole, it occurred to him that the man was Miller. He looked older, his face was tanned, his hair grey and short. But surely, he thought, that's who it was?

Frank dropped the cloth, leaving the tap running, and crossed to the door. It was locked. He usually did this to discourage late customers. He fumbled with the key, finally pulling the door open and stepped down onto the pavement. A bus was sweeping past. When it had gone, the man, too, had gone. Frank looked to his left and right. He hurried along to where he could see down Lady Lane but there was no sign of him there either. Frank shook his head. Perhaps he had made a mistake. Maybe it hadn't been Miller. Why should he have thought about Miller after all this time? 'Strange how the mind worked,' he said to himself. He went back into the barber's and finished cleaning up.

Frank didn't mention any of this when Theresa came through from the salon. By that time, he was convinced that he'd made a mistake. He was slightly embarrassed that he should have been so sure it *was* Miller. And baffled as to what had brought Miller back into his mind.

✵

The café — which had once been The Bay of Naples and was now called The Blue Sea — was heaving. Sixteen- and seventeen-year-olds from the nearby school flirted over their cokes and milkshakes. Groups of women who'd been shopping chattered like starlings. There was, as always on a Friday afternoon, a queue waiting by the counter. The young couple, arm in arm, at the head of the queue was alert and ready to pounce on the next free table.

Crossland, who owned the café, was a small bristly ex-army man. What most people remember about him is that he was always shouting. He shouted at his wife and he shouted at the waitresses. He shouted at the customers, too, especially if they were students or schoolchildren. That was what Crossland did: he strutted up and down the café in his shiny blue-serge double-breasted suit – something of the peacock about him, as with most small men – and shouted at people.

That being so, no one paid much attention when he began shouting that particular afternoon. Someone was getting it, but then, what was new?

'Hey you, what in God's name you up to?'

He seemed to be shouting at a group of students who'd been arguing.

'Stop that! Right now.'

Suddenly he was charging across the café, pushing between the tables, bumping a waitress so that she scaled a cup of coffee over a woman's shopping.

'You no' hear me?'

One of the students looked up.

'What ye on about?'

But Crossland barged past the students, knocking over a young girl of four or five who landed on her elbow and started to cry.

'Jesus Christ!' he said.

People were turning to look. By now, too, they could smell the petrol.

The man was seated at one of the small tables against the far wall. He had unscrewed the top of a grey army-surplus petrol can and was pouring petrol over himself. Crossland had stopped in front of him, trying to take in what he was seeing. The man raised the can and let the petrol splash gently over his head. He was utterly absorbed in what he was doing, like a priest performing some obscure but necessary ritual. The petrol gleamed in his hair, ran down the sides of his face and over his clothes. He kept his face tilted slightly upwards so that the liquid stayed out of his eyes. The petrol soaked greedily into the cloth of his dark blue overcoat.

After a moment, the man said, 'I'm sorry.'

'What?'

Crossland had heard. But he hadn't understood.

'Out! Now! D'you no' hear me, you?'

Crossland was shouting again, frightened rather than merely angry. The man was older than Crossland; sixty-two years old, to be precise. Thin and wiry, his hair cut short, almost grey. Despite his age, he looked fit and, if anything, physically stronger than Crossland. His eyes were pale blue and his skin was sunburnt as if he'd been abroad for many years.

He placed the can on the table in front of him. Crossland could tell from the sound it made on the formica that it was empty. The man flicked open the cap of a square metal lighter. He laid his thumb on the small ridged wheel that would strike a spark from the flint. The smell of petrol was overpowering now. People were standing up, scraping the legs of their chairs back across the tiled floor. A chair tipped over and someone swore. Crossland shook his head, still not entirely believing this.

'This place is full of people. Kids.'

'Get them out.'

Chairs clattered. People clambered and scrambled over tables, everyone heading for the door at the same time. Someone screamed. Two men were fighting to get out first and blocking the way for everyone else. The sudden surge of people into the street soon blocked the traffic. Crossland was still inside the café, talking to the man.

'Don't do this, mister. Please . . . What's the matter wi' ye? . . . Come on. Ye cannae be serious . . . Put that down and talk to me.'

The man moved the lighter closer to his coat. Crossland backed away.

When Crossland was almost at the door, the man rolled his thumb down, striking a spark from the flint.

The flame opened like a flower. The man drew the lighter to his chest. There was a moment when nothing happened. And then another moment when the flame leapt from the lighter to the coat, carried on the fumes.

The flame, more blue than yellow, danced out along the creases of the coat where the petrol had collected in the densest concentrations. There was a soft 'frump', surprisingly muted, and the flames enveloped him like a veil. Soon the people outside could hear him screaming and they were moving, running now, away from the café.

*

When Frank heard what had happened, he knew right away that it was Miller. Just as he knew that it had been Miller standing outside the barber's the night before.

Frank closed the shop and phoned Robert Glen, who had retired some years before. Together, they went to the police station and told an inspector what they knew. With the inspector's help, Robert was able to keep things quiet. He could not contemplate Frank being drawn into this. It would get people talking again and no one needed that. Besides, what good would the truth do anyone now?

From what Frank told them, and by checking the local hotels, the police eventually tracked down Miller's wife. And, in due course, his body was sent back to Australia for burial.

✲

Frank went on working in the barber's until the early eighties. Gina had died – 'finally found some peace', as Frank put it – a good four or five years before that. When he retired, Frank returned to Pozzuoli and bought himself a house with a garden and half an acre of vines. His daughter, Theresa, stayed on in Paisley for a few years until her husband suddenly left her, at the age of fifty-four, for one of the young stylists. Not long after that, she sold the salon and moved out to live with Frank.

Frank died in Pozzuoli last year. Theresa's still there, still living in her father's house (as she always describes it). She does two days a week in a little salon on the front. Her son and three grandchildren visit her every summer, the grandchildren often spending the whole school holidays with her.

The building that housed the café has continued to change hands fairly regularly over the years. Within recent memory, it's been a Chinese restaurant and a takeaway pizza place. Currently, it's a kebab house run by two Armenian brothers. They did well when they stayed open late on Friday and Saturday nights, but were getting too much trouble from kids out of their heads on drink or drugs. Since they've been closing earlier they've barely been covering their costs. So they've decided to try their hand at something else. Right now, there's a 'FOR SALE' sign in the window.

The hairdressers' and barber's in the west end is still there, too, but not for much longer. Theresa's son, who works at the University in Glasgow, went there recently when he heard that the block was coming down. The red leather barber's chair in which he sat for his haircut was the same one in which he'd sat almost thirty years before when his grandfather cut his hair. The barber is a fairly old man who never knew Frank. He rents out the room from the woman who owns the hairdressers' and says that he's retiring when the place closes. The shop itself hasn't changed in years. As the barber said, 'No way was I spending any money on this, no' if it wasnae mine.' There are a couple of pictures on the walls, mostly of Scotland, the usual acres of mountains and heather. But there's one that patently isn't Scottish. It's a fairly old, hand-coloured photograph that hangs to the right of the very fifties coat pegs just as you come in the door. It shows a wide, blue bay surrounded by grey, distant mountains. There are a few ships and smaller boats dotted here and there on the restless water. In the background, there's the unmistakable shape of Vesuvius. When the barber saw Theresa's son looking at the picture as he was putting on his coat, he said, 'Nice auld picture, that.'

'Aye.'

'It was here when I took the place over. Quite liked it, so I left it there. It's about a' I'll take fae here when I go.'

He was sweeping up the hair from the floor. And he came over and stood before the picture with the brush still in his hand.

'I always wondered where it was.'

'The Bay of Naples,' Theresa's son said.

'You reckon?'

'Oh aye,' he said. 'Definitely.'

ALAN CLEWS was born and grew up in Paisley and now lives in London. He's written several plays for television and many episodes of well-known television programmes such as *Lovejoy*, *Love Hurts* and *Shine on Harvey Moon*. He is the author of one other novel, *A Child Of Air*.